NOT ON FIFTH STREET

NOT ON FIFTH STREET

KATHY CANNON WIECHMAN

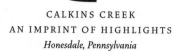

CALKINS CREEK
AN IMPRINT OF HIGHLIGHTS
Honesdale, Pennsylvania

For information about permission to reproduce selections from this
book, please contact permissions@highlights.com.

Calkins Creek
An Imprint of Highlights
815 Church Street
Honesdale, Pennsylvania 18431
Printed in the United States of America

ISBN: 978-1-62979-804-2 (hc) • 978-1-62979-922-3 (e-book)
Library of Congress Control Number: 2017937781

First edition

10 9 8 7 6 5 4 3 2 1

Designed by Barbara Grzeslo
Titles set in Impact
Text set in Garamond 3

In memory of my father,

Albert J. Cannon,

and

for my daughters,

Kelly and Wendy,

and all caretakers

of those who are "different"

PART ONE
PETE

CHAPTER I

ALL FROM A NAME

If Pete Brinkmeyer expected the usual winter of ice-skating and good-natured snowball fights with his brother, Gus, and best friend, Richie Weber, he was in for a huge disappointment. If he hoped for a heavy snowfall, so he and Richie could earn money shoveling sidewalks, those hopes would be drowned as well. It would be a January for the record books.

The year 1937 began innocently enough, and the storm brewing at New Year's dinner wasn't Pete's fault. Not entirely. If Gus needed someone to blame, he should look in the mirror. Gus was the one who'd invited a girl to New Year's dinner in the first place.

Gus had never done something like that before, but Gus didn't act much like Gus lately. He talked on the telephone until the party-line people complained, and he never had time for Pete anymore.

Dad had told Pete not to worry that Gus was mooning

over a girl. It came with being fifteen and a high-school sophomore.

Pete was a freshman, fourteen months younger than Gus. He liked girls, too. But he didn't like any girl enough to invite her home for dinner. Especially New Year's dinner. With Aunt Mary and the whole family.

Traditionally, January 1 was a family day for the Brinkmeyers. Mass in the morning at Saint Joe's, followed by brunch at Aunt Mary's house. Aunt Mary baked coffee cakes that would make Pope Pius condone the deadly sin of gluttony.

The Great Depression that had enveloped the entire country in the last several years had hit Dad's widowed sister hard, and Pete knew Dad slipped her money to "keep the wolf from the door," as he put it.

Aunt Mary provided New Year's brunch, but the family always brought her to their house for dinner. A holiday dinner. In the *dining room!*

Mom had added roasted catfish to the customary baked ham and potatoes this year. It was the only way Aunt Mary had agreed to be there. After all, January 1 of 1937 fell on a Friday.

Even though the bishop had granted a special holy-day dispensation from meatless Friday, Aunt Mary said, "I haven't eaten meat on Friday in my entire life, and I'm not going to start now."

Fish for a holiday dinner was only the beginning of a very different New Year's Day. What had Gus been thinking, inviting Venus Marlowe to a *family* dinner? *This* family dinner?

Four-year-old Timmy stared at Venus from the minute she walked in. The girl wore lipstick, for crying out loud!

"Are you a girl?" Timmy asked. "Or a lady?"

And seven-year-old Etta kept trying to touch the blonde curls that swirled around Venus's head like a halo.

But it was Pete who started the uproar. Unintentionally.

He asked innocent questions, polite ones. "Are you in Gus's class at Saint Joe's? Do you have Sister Ignatius for English?"

Gus answered for Venus. "She's not in my class. She doesn't go to Saint Joe's. She doesn't even live in Ironton. She lives across the river in Russell."

"Doris Stowe in my bridge club lives in Russell," Mom said. "She belongs to Holy Family parish in Ashland."

Russell and Ashland were on the Kentucky side of the Ohio River, just a bridge away from Ironton, Ohio, where the Brinkmeyers lived.

Pete didn't understand the hard look in Gus's eyes, usually meant as a signal to shut his trap, but Pete hadn't said a single embarrassing word about his brother. It wasn't like the time he'd told all the boys on the Knights baseball team that Gus's real name was Augustine.

But thoughts swirling in Pete's head had a way of coming out his mouth. "Is Venus your real name? Is there a Saint Venus? Or were you named for the planet?"

Venus smiled at Pete's questions. "I was named for a famous Greek statue called Venus de Milo, but my mom calls me Venus de Marlowe." Venus giggled a nervous laugh while Gus's stare dang-near burned a hole right through the bridge of Pete's nose.

"Named for a statue. Did you hear that, Mary?" Mom asked, as though Aunt Mary weren't sitting right there the whole time.

"At least they didn't name you Aphrodite." Dad winked at Venus when he said it.

"Who's Aphrodite?" Etta asked.

Pete had wondered the same thing but didn't want to ask and sound ignorant.

"Aphrodite is another name for the pagan goddess Venus," Aunt Mary told her.

Etta's eyes opened wide like a frog's as Aunt Mary's hand fluttered through a quick sign of the cross.

Pagan goddess? Holy saints and sinners! Pete thought. Priests went to foreign countries to convert pagans. Sister Ignatius collected pennies in a jar on her desk to adopt pagan babies. Pagans were to be prayed for, not named after.

The whole family knew Aunt Mary's feelings about religion, including her opinion on names. Babies were to be named after saints. Names not duly canonized were not considered. Amen.

Pete had spoken without thinking, but Mom had goaded Aunt Mary. And now Gus looked as though his head might explode. Pete didn't know anything about ancient gods and goddesses anyway. He needed to switch the conversation to a safer subject.

"Do you know Frankie Bauman?" he asked Venus. "He goes to school at Holy Family?"

"I don't go to Holy Family," she answered. "I go to Russell County High. I'm not Catholic."

Aunt Mary gasped and crossed herself again.

"I see," Mom said. "We say grace before we pass the food, but you don't need to join in if you don't want to."

"I may not be Catholic," Venus said, a slight edge to her voice, "but Catholics aren't the only folks who say grace. Me and my mom pray all the time."

Pete liked Venus's bold attitude, but he knew it wouldn't sit well with his parents and Aunt Mary. He hadn't intended for his innocent question to cause his strict Catholic family to rain judgment down on poor Venus. And he sure didn't mean to cause the flood that came next.

CHAPTER 2

DINNER

The next question came from Etta. "What about your dad? Doesn't he pray, too?"

"My father doesn't live with us. I haven't seen him in years. Him and my mom are divorced."

Etta's open mouth made her frog eyes look small, and Pete was almost certain he heard Aunt Mary fishing in her pocket for her rosary beads.

"What's *'vorced*?" asked Timmy.

"Hush," Aunt Mary told him.

It might have been the hurt look on Venus's face, but Mom turned sweeter than the lone candy cane still hanging on the Christmas tree. She heaped enough ham on Venus's plate to feed the whole family—and a camp of hobos at the rail yard. Mom's answer to every problem was food.

The table grew painfully quiet. Dad said the ham was good, and Mom nodded. They both ignored Aunt Mary's disapproving look before she asked Gus to pass the fish.

Pete tried to concentrate on eating, but this wasn't the usual Brinkmeyer family meal. Dad didn't make his typical January-first remark about hoping the new calendar had more Saturdays on it. And nobody mentioned the warm January weather that was already turning December's snow into slush.

When Pete looked at Gus, he saw the way Gus clenched and unclenched his jaw, saw his narrowed eyes and hard stare. Nobody else seemed to notice, but Pete had never seen his brother so mad. It was worse than telling his real name to the Knights. Worse than the time he'd made paper airplanes out of Gus's algebra homework. Worse than the time he'd smashed a cow's eye on the railroad track to make Lucy Handorf squeal—and Gus had squealed louder.

A bite of potato caught in Pete's throat. He tried to cough it up as silently as he could, but potato wasn't the only thing choking him. His brother's anger was like a snake coiling around Pete's windpipe.

Dad clapped Pete firmly on the back, dislodging the potato, which hurtled across the table and plunked into Aunt Mary's coffee cup.

~~~

Gus went with Dad to drive Venus and Aunt Mary home, and Pete handed delicate glass ornaments to Mom to wrap carefully and pack away for next year. Mom treasured these ornaments passed down from her mother, so Pete was extra

15

mindful with them. The bottle-cap ornaments he and Gus had made years ago were tossed carelessly into a round Quaker Oats box.

Timmy was too young to un-decorate the tree, and Etta was only allowed to take down the paper chains she had made from old magazine pages.

"Mom," Etta said, "Christmas is over, but my birthday is in two months. Can I get lipstick for my birthday? I'll be eight."

"For heaven's sake, Etta. I didn't wear lipstick until my high school graduation."

"You mean they *had* lipstick back in the old days?"

"1917 was *not* the old days," Mom said.

Timmy looked up from pushing his toy train across the rug. "What's *'vorced*, Mommy?"

"It's a grown-up word," Mom said.

"Is it a cuss word?"

In this house, it might as well be, Pete thought.

Mom grabbed the last candy cane from the tree and gave it to Timmy. "Eat this in the kitchen. You go with him, Etta."

"How come Timmy gets the last candy cane?" Etta whined.

"You'll get a swat on your hind end if you don't mind me," Mom said.

After the little ones scurried from the living room, Mom asked, "Pete, how long has your brother been seeing this

Venus girl?" Mom said the word *Venus* as though the girl had come from another planet.

"I don't know. He never talks to me anymore," Pete said. "I asked him to see the new *Three Stooges* picture at the Lyric with me two Saturdays ago, but he'd already seen it. Saw it with her, I guess." Pete nearly dropped a star-shaped ornament as the sting from Gus's refusal rushed back.

Mom shook her head. "Your father and I need to discuss this Venus situation."

Pete picked up the Quaker Oats box again and heard bottle caps clinking together. He and Gus had searched for different kinds. Coca-Cola. Pepsi-Cola. Hires Root Beer. Vernor's Ginger Ale. They were just silly ornaments, but nine-year-old Pete and ten-year-old Gus had made them with pride. Together.

CHAPTER 3

BROTHERS

Apparently, Mom had discussed the "Venus situation" with Dad. And the two of them discussed it with Gus.

Pete heard their voices drift up the stairs to the second-floor back bedroom he shared with Gus. Mom's tone was firm and Dad's was insistent, but Gus's was defiant. Pete couldn't make out the words, but he knew how his parents felt about Gus keeping company with a Protestant girl.

A few women in their tightly knit German Catholic community still frowned on Mom because she was *Irish* Catholic. Protestants were strictly *verboten*. Forbidden. And divorce was something only spoken about in whispers and gossip.

Pete looked out the window, trying not to listen to the voices as they grew louder. A dark shadow prowled around the garage at the edge of the yard. A raccoon or Mrs. Taylor's creepy cat? It didn't matter. It was something other than that conversation in the kitchen.

Dad's words could be gruff, and his look of disappointment could cut to the bone. Mom wielded justice quickly and quietly, and when she put her foot down, she was immovable. Pete didn't want Gus to go through that.

The voices stopped and footsteps bounded up the stairs. Gus stormed into the room. "Why can't you keep your nose out of my business?" His voice was a harsh whisper. "Venus is a nice girl, and you embarrassed her. Now Mom and Dad don't want me to see her anymore."

Pete whispered back, "I didn't mean to. I was just trying to make conversation like normal people do. If you'da told me you'd gone all moon-eyed over a *Protestant*, I'da kept your secret. But you didn't tell me there was a secret to keep."

"No secret now, thanks to you, you double-crossing stool pigeon. Just stay out'a my life, Petey." Gus turned his back on Pete and pulled his pajamas from under his pillow.

"Don't call me Petey!"

Gus turned and pulled himself up to his full height, a good two inches taller than Pete. He looked down at his brother. "You don't have the sense God gave a tadpole, *Petey*."

The remark stung. Maybe Pete wasn't as smart as Gus when it came to books and schoolwork, but common sense was a different matter.

Even though Gus was taller, Pete outweighed him by at least twenty pounds. Twenty pounds of muscle. Pete doubled his fists. He was tempted to prove that sometimes stronger was better than smarter, but he bit back angry words and went down the hall to the bathroom. He'd give his brother time to get over his anger—and Venus Marlowe. He had to get over her. Mom and Dad had issued their verdict.

CHAPTER 4

RAIN

The weather was warm for an Ironton January. Slushy puddles lined the curbs, and snow melted on winter lawns, streaming water into brick streets. It was January 4 and the first day of school since Christmas vacation.

"Think there'll be a flood this year?" Pete asked, skirting a puddle, as he, Gus, and Richie Weber walked home from school. Floods in the Ohio River Valley were common, especially in Ironton's lowlands.

"Probably." It was the first word Gus had spoken to him since New Year's, and it likely had slipped out by accident. But Pete latched onto it, hoping Gus was beginning to melt, too.

"Think it'll get as high as last year?" Pete hoped for another accidental word.

But it was Richie who answered. "I hope not. Last year we dragged everything upstairs from the basement to keep it dry. We got almost three feet of water down there. When the flood drained off, the basement stunk worse than when we found that dead dog up by the cemetery."

Richie's family lived on Second Street near the liquor store where his dad worked. Just two blocks from the Ohio River. The Brinkmeyer house on Fifth Street had never experienced a flood. Five blocks from the river, that was unheard of.

"Pop says they got lots of snow upriver last month," Richie went on. "This warm spell is gonna melt it and send it our way."

"You've toughed out floods before," Gus said.

"Yeah," Richie agreed. "Floods and the Depression and whatever kettle of fish God throws our way." Richie laughed. "Maybe next time He'll batter and fry them fish for us."

Richie's dad had been out of work for five years before the job at the liquor store opened. Life had been rough for them, but the fish joke was the closest Richie ever came to complaining.

"Call me if you need me," Pete said. And he meant it.

~~~

On Tuesday, Pete listened to *Fibber McGee and Molly* on the radio with Dad and Gus. The show came on at 9:30, and Mom bestowed a special Tuesday dispensation from the boys' usual school-night bedtime. Pete thought being told when to go to bed was for little kids anyway.

Mom came in from the kitchen. "You boys didn't open any windows upstairs, did you?" she asked. "It's starting to rain."

"I didn't," Gus said.

"Not me," added Pete. "Richie Weber won't be happy about rain. He's worried there's gonna be a flood."

"It wouldn't surprise me," Dad said. "Floods in Ironton are like ants at a picnic. You can't stop them. Houses near the river—like Richie's—get the brunt. Last year, most of those houses had water in their basements. That kind of flood is a nuisance, but back in 1913, those houses were underwater. Just roof peaks sticking out."

Pete tried to imagine the river high enough to cover most of Richie's house.

"Folks on Ironton's riverfront are used to floods," Dad said. "When I was a boy, there wasn't a family between Second Street and the river that didn't keep a rowboat handy. It was the only way of getting around when the water came up."

"Could it come up to Fifth Street?" Pete asked.

Gus gave him a condescending look.

Dad chuckled. "Not a chance, not way up here. Besides, record-breaking floods like 1913 are mighty unusual, and even the flood of '13 couldn't touch us here."

Pete lay awake that night, listening to the thrum of rain on the shingled roof, thinking about floods and Richie Weber. "It's January," he said out loud. "We should get snow, not rain."

Gus was as silent as an unplugged radio.

CHAPTER 5

AND
MORE RAIN

The only thing as persistent as Gus's grudge was rain. On Wednesday, it poured all day. Thursday was more of the same.

After school on Thursday, Pete stopped to fetch the empty garbage can from the curb, while Gus strode up the drive to the back of the house. They always used the back door when it rained or snowed, to keep wet boot prints off the living room rug.

Gus didn't help with the can, didn't offer to carry Pete's books inside. Pete hadn't heard more than four words from Gus all week. And half those words had been *Petey*. How long would Gus stay mad? Over a girl, for crying out loud?

While Pete stewed, he failed to see Mr. Geswein's Chevrolet heading up Fifth Street. The car splashed through a puddle, sending up a spray that soaked one leg of Pete's trousers and sloshed down inside his boot.

"Sorry, Pete," the neighbor called as he turned into his driveway next door.

Pete waved. "No harm done." A smile for Mr. Geswein hid unspoken grumbles against Gus.

Leaving the garbage can in its place beside the back door, Pete stepped into the sunroom. Rain beaded up and formed little rivers that streamed down the outside of the windowed walls. Pete tugged off his boots and shoes, peeled off the wet sock, and carried it upstairs to hang over the bathtub.

With one sock on, he traipsed down the hall to his bedroom, where Gus sat at the homework desk, pencil in hand, scrawling words onto paper. Gus couldn't spare a single word for his brother, but on paper, words poured out like spilled milk.

Maybe this was Gus's way of ending the feud. Gus wrote stories about G-men, bootleggers, and gangsters, and Pete always waited eagerly for the next installment.

"What'cha writing?" Pete asked. "A shoot-'em-up with Tommy guns, gun molls, and hit men?"

Gus sprawled both elbows across the page so Pete couldn't see. "Nothing for your eyes."

"Come on, Gus. When are you gonna stop holding this Venus thing against me? We're brothers, and blood is thicker than . . . than. . . perfume."

"Cain and Abel were brothers, too," Gus said. "You know how that turned out." He folded his paper, shoved it in a book, and hurried from the room as if Pete were plotting to recreate the Biblical Cain-killed-Abel scene right there in their bedroom.

25

Pete dropped onto the chair Gus had just vacated. His algebra homework was going to be an uphill battle without Gus's help. Sister Josepha expected students to read a chapter and work the problems at the end of it, but Pete needed someone to explain it to him. And Gus had always been that someone.

~~~

On Friday morning, Pete looked out his upstairs window to see the wet spindly arms of Mrs. Taylor's walnut tree reaching toward a dreary gray sky. Rain again.

Gus was dressed for school, while Pete still wore pajamas. Before the New Year's incident, Gus would have goaded Pete to hurry, maybe even thrown a wet towel at his head. Today, nothing.

At breakfast, the hum of the Kelvinator refrigerator competed with the sound of rain on the windows of the sunroom, where the family ate most of their meals. A few years ago, Pete had helped Dad build a picnic table inside the sunroom. Benches sat against opposite walls, and the room was almost all table. If someone slid in after you, there was no getting up again until that person did.

Dressed for his job at the post office, Dad came through the doorway from the kitchen, where the almost-never-closed door was held in place with a cat-shaped iron doorstop. Standing in the small space at the end of the table, Dad looked out the sunroom's glass door and scanned the sky.

26

As he sat down beside Pete, he grinned. "Think we need to build us an ark, Pete?"

Pete grinned back. "You get the lumber, and I'll fetch the toolbox."

Gus said nothing. Gus didn't care about building or fixing. He probably couldn't name half the tools in Dad's toolbox.

Pete, on the other hand, had always been curious about how things were built and what made things work. When he was six years old, he took apart Grandma Walsh's cuckoo clock to see what made the bird pop out. He had put it back together again—mostly—but the cuckoo's call had never sounded quite the same.

After that, Dad let Pete help when he worked around the house. He showed Pete which wrench to hand him to loosen the drain plug when they changed the oil in the Buick. He'd even lifted eight-year-old Pete to let him turn the slip wrench on the oil filter. Dad used to call Pete his "Deputy Mechanic."

Now Pete could change the oil filter by himself, and Dad relied on him to help keep both the Buick and the house in good working order. Those things were so much easier than algebra.

It never seemed to bother Gus that Dad worked on things with Pete instead of him. After all, Gus had his writing. He said he would rather "build with words."

Pete watched Gus's face across the breakfast table. Gus didn't look up from his Cream of Wheat, but Pete sensed that the clenching of his brother's jaw had nothing to do with eating.

CHAPTER 6

THE RIVER

When they left school that Friday afternoon, Richie Weber said, "Sister Basil liked my history report, Gus. When you made me see history as real people doing things, it got easier."

Sure, Gus had time to help Richie with history, but Sister Josepha had marked up Pete's algebra homework with her red pencil until it looked to be bleeding to death.

Richie went on in a serious tone, "Soon as I get home, me and Pop are gonna move stuff up from the basement."

"Your basement flooded?" Gus asked. He talked to Richie as though Pete weren't there.

"Not yet," Richie said, "but Pop says it's sure as flies in summer if this rain keeps up. He says we gotta be ready."

Rain drizzled down the back of Pete's collar. "Can I help?" he asked. Why hurry home to be taunted by the name *Petey*? Or even worse, to have Gus act like his brother didn't exist?

"I'd give you a hand, Richie," Gus said, "but I have a mountain of homework."

Yeah, right, Pete thought, as if Gus couldn't obliterate that mountain in minutes. Gus just plain didn't want to do anything with Pete. Pete remembered how he, Gus, and Richie had done everything together not so long ago. Up until that day in October when Gus had met Venus. How could Gus ignore Richie now, just to spite Pete?

~~~

As they neared Richie's house on Second Street, Pete could see the brown, murky water of the Ohio just beyond the railroad tracks. A little more rain and those tracks would be *under* water.

"It's muddier than I've ever seen it," Pete said.

"From all that runoff upriver," Richie said. "Makes me wonder how they got any ground left up in Pittsburgh, the way it washes down here. You think the river's muddy. You should see what it leaves behind after it floods the basement."

~~~

Pete helped Richie and his dad lug boxes up steep basement steps and pile them in the dining room. Pete and Richie carried heavy ones together, Richie bent like a horseshoe backing up the steps, while Pete bore most of the weight from the bottom. He hoped Richie didn't lose his footing and fall. He didn't want to wind up smashed like a bug on the basement floor.

Back in the basement, Mr. Weber pointed to an old hot

plate on a high shelf. "Can you reach that, Pete? If gas shuts off, we'll need it for cooking. We'll use the fireplace for heat."

"My dad said this whole house would have been underwater back in 1913," Pete said.

"It dang-near was," Mr. Weber said. "I was just a boy at the time, but when we bought this house from the Carters, Mr. Carter showed us a photograph. A rowboat was tied up by a second-story window. I hope to never see another flood like that."

Richie's mom stirred soup at the stove, as Pete set the hot plate in the kitchen. Not only did the soup look watery, but the kitchen shelves were bare compared to the pantry at home.

Mom had canned all summer just like every year. Her pantry shelves were well-stocked with bread-and-butter pickles, apple butter, jellies, ketchup, beans, carrots, most anything a growing boy might need. But the Brinkmeyers hadn't been hit hard by the Depression the way Richie's family was.

Richie set a box on the kitchen table, flexed his fingers, and cracked his knuckles. Richie always cracked his knuckles when he was nervous.

Walking to the door, Pete told his friend again, "You can call me if you need anything. You know that, right?"

Richie nodded.

Pete didn't go straight home. The river seemed to pull him closer, almost to the water's edge. He needed a good look at the mighty Ohio, which caused so much concern for Richie's family. He had offered to help, but what could he do?

Along the banks, rain dimpled the water's muddy surface the way it did in puddles. But out in its middle, the river surged like a fierce animal, whipping into waves that rose and hurried downriver. A tangle of branches floated past, carried in the swift current. Were they branches from an Ironton tree? Or had they traveled all the way from Pittsburgh?

Pete looked at houses and imagined them with muddy water up to second-floor windows and people using rowboats to go places. He and Dad had fished on the river before. But that river was nothing like this wild, alive one. He hurried away as though it might reach out and grab him.

CHAPTER 7

SOGGY SUNDAY

A wet Saturday was followed by a soggy Sunday. Gray skies and relentless rain. Pete stood by the front window, watching rain ping off the brick street, puddle on the sidewalk, pummel the last remnants of snow from the sodden grass, and drench the leafless limbs of the Norway maple that stood near the curb. So much water. How did the wild river look today?

Etta always took longest to get ready for church. Just how much primping did a seven-year-old need to do? Pete's stomach rumbled, but breakfast had to wait until after Mass. Church law.

"Etta!" Dad used his I-mean-now voice.

"In a minute," she called for the third time.

The rain showed no sign of stopping, and Pete dreaded a day of being trapped inside with nothing to do but read the Sunday funnies. He and Dad couldn't work on anything. Not on Sunday.

If Gus weren't still mad, they could play checkers. Gus

33

usually won, but it was better than doing nothing. Jack Benny would come on the radio at seven o'clock, but there would be an eon full of empty hours before that.

Etta finally came downstairs, the scent of Mom's cologne trailing in her wake. Mom yanked her into the kitchen by the arm and scrubbed Etta's face and neck with a kitchen rag.

"I don't know what's gotten into you, young lady, but it had better stop. And now!"

Dad had already backed the Buick from the garage to the sunroom door. He gave the horn an impatient tap.

During the drive to Sunday Mass, the windshield wipers flapped with a *thwack!* A clear spot appeared on the glass, only to be swallowed again by a stream of rain until the next *thwack* cleared it again. Pete kept his nose pressed to the window to avoid the strong smell exuding from his sister.

Dad sniffed. "Did you maybe go a little overboard with the Prince Matchabelli, Ruth?" He cranked down his window halfway.

"That's not me," Mom answered. "It's your daughter."

"Etta!" Dad said sternly, as Etta slid lower in the seat.

Rain from Dad's open window spattered Pete's face, but the fresh air, in all its wetness, smelled good. How could the same water that cleaned the air turn the Ohio into a muddy force?

Dad stopped the Buick in front of Saint Joseph Church at the corner of Adams and Third. Mom opened an umbrella

34

and ushered the kids beneath it while Pete and Gus splashed up the steps and waited for Dad to park the car.

From the vestibule, Pete saw servers lighting candles and heard the organist practicing. Gus, Pete, Etta, and Timmy had all been baptized in this church when they were babies. Augustine, Peter, Mary Etta, and Timothy. All named for saints. Just like God and Aunt Mary intended.

The smell of wet clothing, a smell stronger than Etta, hung in the air like incense. Pete looked at the other parishioners. Nobody's umbrella seemed to have been up to the task. Coats had wet shoulders, and hair hung damp and limp.

Pete felt a drop of water slither from his hair down the back of his neck as he bent his knee in a quick genuflect before sliding into the pew. He didn't drop his knee all the way to the floor because the aisle was puddled from wet feet.

Mass began, and Father Gloekner spoke the Latin words Pete had heard all his life. He knew them by heart, as well as their English translations. He recited the responses along with everyone else but found his mind wandering.

A stained-glass window towered above the statue of Saint Joseph holding the Christ Child. Pete had often watched the window's colors appear like confetti on churchgoers' faces. A green or orange speck might dance along someone's forehead and jump to a nose. But without sunlight, the colors stayed dull and lifeless on the window. Just like all of Ironton.

Three-year-old Stevie Hobart stood on a front pew in

soaked pants, which Pete suspected had nothing to do with rain. If the boy had left a puddle on the pew, a Hobart parent or sibling was in for a soggy shock.

As the sermon neared, when everyone would sit, Pete held in a laugh. Looking across the top of Etta's head at Gus, he cleared his throat to get Gus's attention, but Gus didn't give him a glance. The *old* Gus would have noticed the Hobart situation and shot Pete a smirk.

It had been more than a week since New Year's dinner. Was Gus going to hold a grudge forever?

In the vestibule after Mass, Dad talked with some of the other men. Pete edged closer to hear what their serious-toned voices said. He was only able to catch a few words. *West End. River levels. Flood.* The concerned looks on the men's faces reminded Pete of the ferocious river he had seen on Friday. The river so close to Richie's house. In the West End!

~~~

The family slid into the Buick when Dad pulled it to the curb. "Something needs to be done about this rain," Dad said.

Like what? Nobody could make rain stop.

"We need to protect people and their property," Dad said.

"But how?" Pete asked.

Dad didn't answer as he pulled the car into Third Street's after-Mass traffic. Crossing Adams Street, the car in front slowed, and Dad stopped in the middle of the intersection.

"Look at that." Dad pointed in the direction of the river.

Pete's head turned. The water was much higher than when he'd gone to Richie's house just two days ago. The far end of Adams Street disappeared right into the wild, muddy Ohio.

CHAPTER 8

PICTURE SHOW

After school on Monday, Pete told Richie, "I saw how high the river was after church yesterday."

"No water in our basement yet," Richie assured him, "and the forecasters on the radio don't think it'll get as high as last year. But Pop is fussing up a storm. He says water can rise quicker than you can say 'Franklin Delano Roosevelt' and catch you unawares."

The rain didn't stop. Tuesday marked a full week of rainy days. On Wednesday Pete quit counting.

By Friday, Richie said there were a few inches of water in his basement, and still rising. "But they say on the radio we're gonna get a cold snap," he said. "That'll slow it down."

~~~

Saturday morning *was* cold. Pete took some change from his sock drawer. "I'm going to the picture show with Richie," he told Gus. "You want to go with us?"

Gus shook his head. Two long weeks since New Year's

dinner and Pete was still getting the cold shoulder. He'd hated it when Gus spent so much time with Venus, but now Venus's absence was more intrusive than her presence had been.

Pete told Mom he was meeting Richie at the Lyric. The picture was *Klondike Annie*, starring Mae West. He didn't mention the star's name to Mom. She didn't think Mae West was the kind of actress a young boy should see, which made Pete want to see her all the more.

Mom handed Pete a dime to pick up a loaf of bread on his way home. "The bread I baked last week is gone, so we'll eat store-bought until I bake again on Monday. Use the extra penny to buy candy for Etta and Timmy since they've been stuck in the house all week."

As he started out the door, Mom said, "Gus isn't going with you?"

"Gus doesn't want to do anything with me anymore."

Mom patted his shoulder. "He'll get over her. Just give him a little more time."

Pulling his coat collar up against his neck, Pete hurried through the rain. Thin sheets of ice floated on puddles hugging the curb. When he and Gus were little squirts, they'd jumped into ice-covered puddles, breaking the surface and splashing water in all directions. Sometimes Pete missed being a little kid. And doing things with Gus.

The Lyric was on Second Street, and Pete got there early.

He thought about going to the riverbank again while he waited for Richie. Just to see. But the spot he'd stood on to see the river last week was *underneath* the river now.

"Water's deeper in the basement," Richie said, while they stood in line to buy tickets. "But not as high as last year. Pop says this chill will do the trick."

Pete held out his hands palms up. "You're not scared?"

"Nah, Pop and me been through floods before." Richie tried to sound fearless, but Pete had known him too long to believe it. And, during the picture, Richie's knuckle-cracking sounded like corn popping.

~~~

When the picture was over, Pete pulled on his gloves as they joined the crowd that spilled from the doorway.

"Pop says they cut out parts of the picture because they were too steamy," Richie said, his breath hanging visibly in the air. "I'd like to get a peek at those scenes." Tucking his hands under his arms to keep out the cold, he raised his eyebrows. "I bet that'd warm me up."

As Richie turned toward home, Pete wanted to convince him not to worry, but if Richie wouldn't admit his fears, what could Pete say? Especially when Pete felt the fear was well-grounded.

"Keep your feet dry," he called over his shoulder as he headed for Wally's Corner Store. *What a nitwitted thing to say,* he berated himself. But he had told Richie repeatedly to call him if he needed him. What else could he do? Just wait for that call?

Wally's was crowded, even for a Saturday. Wally and his wife were behind the counter, and both had lines of people waiting to pay.

"Might not get out of my house for groceries if my street floods," one man said. "I need to stock up."

Pete grabbed the second-last loaf of Wonder Bread from the shelf and wondered what people who couldn't afford to stock up would do. He remembered that well-stocked pantry at home. Maybe Pete could sneak out a few jars of food to Richie.

During the height of the Depression, Pete had often shared his packed school lunches with Richie, but this felt different. He had to help Richie without hurting his feelings.

CHAPTER 9

WOMEN AND CHILDREN BEHIND

The cold snap that was expected to keep the river in check lasted only one day.

After Mass on Sunday, Dad talked with the men in the vestibule again, and once more, talk was about the river.

As the Buick crossed Adams, Pete's eyes followed Dad's. The river was much closer than last week, and its water carried more than branches. Pete saw a gate, a bicycle wheel, and what looked like an outhouse riding in the strong current.

"Some of the men are going to the West End to fill and pile sandbags," Dad said as he headed the car toward home. "That end of town will be hit hard if the river goes much higher. We want to get a handle on it before it rises too much."

This was good, Pete thought. The men from Saint Joe's were going to do something to help Richie's family and other folks on the riverfront. Maybe Dad would let him go along.

Dad looked over his shoulder. "Gus, I want you to come with me and help."

"Me?" Gus said. "Really?"

"Gus?" Pete said. "What about me? Gus doesn't know which end of a shovel to hold."

"That's enough, Pete." Dad's tone was sharp. "You stay home with your mother."

~~~

Gus changed into work clothes while Pete sat on the edge of his bed. Dad was in his own bedroom getting ready, so Pete kept his voice low. "I don't see why he's taking you. I'm the one who always helps him."

"Maybe he needs someone with a brain this time," Gus said.

Pete jumped up. "You wiseacre, I'll pound your brains onto this floor." *Or at least knock that smug look off your face,* he thought. Pete had been hoping Gus would talk to him, but this wasn't the kind of talking he'd wished for.

What was Dad thinking? Pete had been Dad's Deputy Mechanic since he was a little squirt. And filling sandbags didn't even require a mechanic, just a strong back and hands. Pete had that over Gus any day.

Gus rolled a spare pair of socks into one pocket and spare underwear into the other. "Dad said we might stay down there overnight and sleep on cots in the American Legion hall." Gus made it sound like a camping trip instead of hard work. Didn't he realize not coming home overnight meant working well past dark and beginning again at dawn? Pete could handle that. But Gus?

"What about school?" Pete asked.

"I can catch up on anything I miss," Gus said. "I'm always way ahead of my class anyhow."

True, Gus did better in school than Pete, but that had nothing to do with filling sandbags. "It makes no sense," Pete said. "Why *you*?"

"I guess they need *men* to help," Gus said. "Women and children stay behind."

Women and children! Anger rose in Pete's throat. "You louse." He doubled his fists. This time, he surely would have taken a swing at Gus, but he heard footsteps on the stairs. Mom appeared in the doorway.

"I packed sandwiches for you and Dad," she told Gus. "Go grab a quick bite of breakfast before you head out."

"See you later, *Petey*." Gus edged past Mom.

"Go chase yourself," Pete muttered under his breath as Gus galloped downstairs.

"Come eat breakfast, Pete," Mom said, before heading down the stairs.

Dad came down the hall from his front bedroom and stopped in Pete's doorway. "I don't know how long this will take, Pete," he said. "Feed the furnace while I'm gone. And anything else that needs doing."

Pete nodded, knowing if he spoke, disappointment and anger would spill out.

When Dad started down the steps, Pete grumbled in a hushed voice, "I'll be here with the *children*."

"Don't let me down, Pete," Dad called.

Pete didn't want to make Dad mad, even though Dad had betrayed him. Pete couldn't bear to sit across the table from Gus's satisfied smirk or watch Dad drive away without him. He didn't go down to breakfast until he heard the Buick back out of the drive.

CHAPTER 10

RISING
WORRIES

Several older boys also missed school on Monday, gone to help in the West End. Everybody seemed to be helping but Pete.

Pete sat in biology class, looking at pictures of frogs without their skin, wondering what he had done to make Dad choose Gus over him. Surely it couldn't have been the New Year's incident. But what other sin had he committed?

In the cafeteria at lunch, Pete pulled a ham sandwich from the sack Mom had packed. Were Gus and Dad eating ham sandwiches at the American Legion hall? They hadn't come home last night.

"The water's getting pretty deep in our basement," Richie said. "Almost as bad as last year."

Richie's words hit Pete like a punch to the gut. He had nearly forgotten Richie's troubles after Dad had taken Gus to help. "You could stay with us," Pete said. "Gus's bed is empty."

"I'll stay with Pop. He won't leave our house. We ain't

got much, but Pop's not about to let some scalawag break in and traipse off with it. Mom'll stay with Grandma in Coal Grove, but not me and Pop. This ain't our first flood." Richie cracked his knuckles. "We'll be fine, even if the basement fills all the way to the ceiling."

Pete wasn't fooled by Richie's bravado. "Do you think it could rise that much?" he asked.

"Nah, but Pop gave the rowboat a going-over, just in case. Can you imagine? Rowing up to Wally's for a quart of milk?"

"Wally's is clean up on Fourth Street," Pete said. "It'll never get that high."

"I just wish this dang rain would quit," Richie said, dropping his façade at last. "It lets up for an hour or two, and comes back harder than ever. Pop says it's like God pauses just long enough to refill the clouds."

"I wish it would stop, too," Pete said, handing Richie a hardboiled egg. If the rain stopped, Richie and other folks in the West End wouldn't have to worry, Gus and Dad could come home, and Pete could stop feeling so helpless.

But Gus and Dad didn't come home. That night or Tuesday either. Pete shoveled coal into the furnace every morning and again after school. He wasn't going to let Dad down, even though Dad had passed him over for Gus.

At supper, Etta pushed peas around on her plate. "When's Daddy coming home?" she whined. "He's been gone for a month!"

"He's been gone for two days," Mom corrected. She reached over and covered Etta's hand with her own. "There are people who need his help."

"But what about us?" Etta pulled her hand away. "We need him, too!"

"Those folks' homes are in danger of being flooded," Pete said. "You have me and Mom if you need anything, but we don't have to worry about flooding here. Not on Fifth Street."

After Mom put the kids to bed, she and Pete listened to news on the radio.

"Low-lying streets in Ashland, Kentucky, have been closed because of high water," the voice on the radio said. "Some Ohio families have evacuated their riverfront homes and moved their furniture into railroad cars. US Route 52 has been closed between Chesapeake and Cincinnati."

"Mom, do you know where the old rowboat is?" Pete asked.

"I think it's under a tarp behind the garage."

Pete's feeling of helplessness was rising along with the river, and it was time for him to do something. Dad and Gus were being useful. Pete wasn't going to sit back and do nothing. He'd get the rowboat ready to rescue folks on the riverfront.

He'd also take a couple jars of food from the pantry to school tomorrow. He'd tell Richie they had too much or something. Anything! He was tired of doing nothing.

CHAPTER 11

INAUGURATION DAY

Wednesday's rain blew in on a strong wind, sending sheets of water across streets. At school, it lashed windowpanes as students gathered around the radio in Sister Basil's classroom, waiting for the tubes to warm up. Sister Basil was eager to hear President Roosevelt's inauguration speech, but Pete suspected most other minds were on rain and flooding.

The radio crackled to life, as the announcer talked about rain. Even in Washington! The voice said the president was bare-headed in gusty wind and a "deluge."

President Roosevelt talked about one-third of the country still struggling in poverty from the Depression. Pete looked around at those he knew were among that impoverished third. Lucy Handorf's skinny legs showed from beneath a dress at least two sizes too small. Tommy Fritch usually brought nothing but dry crackers in his packed lunch. And Pete remembered the bare shelves in Richie's kitchen.

Dad's post office job and Mom's abundant garden had

kept the Brinkmeyers from suffering the worst hardships of the past years. Pete hadn't thought much about what others had gone through, but now the river was rising. How could these folks make do in a serious flood?

~~~

After school, the wind whipped around Pete and Richie as they headed home.

"I have an idea," Pete said. "We can haul my dad's rowboat down to the flooded areas and take food to people who need it."

"Nifty," Richie agreed. "We can use Pop's rowboat, too."

"And we can rescue folks who don't have their own boat," Pete added.

"Maybe Gus will be back in time to go along?" Richie said.

Pete hoped Gus would be home, but he doubted Gus would help him with anything. That Gus didn't exist anymore.

At home, the wind threatened to knock Pete off his feet and pelted him with rain, as he uncovered the rowboat and dragged it through the garage's open front doors.

Mrs. Taylor's creepy cat zipped inside before he could close the doors. He left one door open for her to skedaddle.

"Scram!" he said, but the cat sat on her haunches, cocking her head to one side, watching him check the boat for leaks. With one orange eye and one blue eye, the cat gave Pete the willies.

He tried to ignore her as he found a small hole and plugged it with a piece of old inner tube, wedging the tube in tightly with the tip of a screwdriver.

By the time he finished, the cat had disappeared. He looked around the garage to make sure she was truly gone before he pushed the door closed and went to the house.

The sweet smell of freshly baked cookies greeted Pete in the sunroom. Tin sheets of gingersnaps and oatmeal cookies sat cooling on the picnic table.

"Don't touch the oatmeal cookies," Mom called from the kitchen. "Those are for Gus."

Pete bit into a warm gingersnap. "Is he coming home?"

Mom bit her lip. "Eventually," she said. "How much longer can they stay gone? I want these cookies ready and waiting when he comes back. You know they're his favorite." She eased a spatula under the cookies and slid them into the cookie tin.

Pete eyed the cookie tin with a smile. Its hand-painted surface was peeling after four years of use. Pete had painted an old cracker tin and Gus had lettered the word *cookies* across it. It had been an apology offering after he and Gus had broken Mom's china cookie jar during a struggle for the last cookie.

Now, Pete would gladly give first, last, and all cookies to Gus, if Gus would come home and things could go back to normal. But the river rose higher every day and threatened people's homes. How could things be normal?

CHAPTER 12

WATER IN THE BASEMENT

Dad and Gus had been gone four days.

Pete watched Mom chew her lip as they listened to news on the radio. Upriver, in Catlettsburg, Kentucky, the riverfront was completely underwater. What did that mean for Ironton?

Maybe Pete and Richie could embark on their plan after school tomorrow. Pete had enough money for a few loaves of bread, and surely Mom would donate some jars of food for a worthy cause. They'd row the boat right up to houses where floodwater lapped at front porches. And Pete would hold back a loaf of bread, a jar of jelly, and some gingersnaps to give Richie when they finished.

~~~

Pete lay in bed, listening to the wind's howl. A door banged. He slipped out of bed and padded downstairs on bare feet. The front door was secure. So was the back door.

He squinted through the sunroom windows, but he

52

couldn't see the garage through the steady rain. He was certain he had left the garage doors closed. *Must'a been a neighbor's door,* Pete thought, and went back upstairs to slide beneath his covers.

No more doors banged, but the wind's ceaseless wail seeped around windows, sounding fierce and angry enough to attack Pete in his bed. Gus's bed, still neatly made since Sunday, was close enough for Pete to touch if he reached out. But he didn't reach out. That way, he could pretend Gus had never left.

Storms had never bothered him when Gus was here.

~~~

On Thursday, Pete was eager to tell Richie the rowboat was ready. But Richie wasn't at school. Was he all right? How deep was the water in the Weber basement? Richie had said they'd stay even if it reached the ceiling. He didn't mean that, did he?

After school, Pete turned toward Second Street. He had to check on Richie. But as he neared Third Street, he could go no further. Third was running with muddy water.

He hurried home, where Mom stood by the open refrigerator. "I was sure I had more meatloaf left than this," she said.

Pete told her about the river. "We need to do something!"

"Second Street is where Dad and Gus went," Mom said and rushed to turn on the radio in the living room. Pete stood beside her. But the radio newsman said nothing about Second Street.

"Hundreds of people in Russell, Kentucky, were evacuated from their homes today," the radio voice said.

"Doesn't that Venus girl live in Russell?" Mom asked.

Pete nodded. "But Gus never told me where in Russell."

"We'll pray for her," Mom suggested. "And for Dad and Gus. Right now that's all we can do."

"And for Richie," Pete added, wanting the radio to say everyone was safe. But it didn't mention Ironton.

"There's no word of casualties," Mom said. "Dad and Gus must be helping flood victims. No news is good news, right?" She didn't look convinced, but she went back to the kitchen.

Casualties? Pete thought. Did that mean dead?

~~~

After Friday supper, Pete warmed up the radio while Mom tucked Timmy and Etta into bed.

The static on the radio was worse than usual, so Pete and Mom scooted close. The fire station was flooded, and its engines had been moved up to Wagner Funeral Home.

Mom shook her head. "It's nearly as bad as 1913."

The radio announcer listed schools to be closed on Monday due to flooding. Nearly every school in Ironton! Even the ones on higher ground, like Whitwell and Kingsbury, were being used as first-aid stations and temporary shelters for those whose homes were flooded. Maybe Richie and his dad would go to one of them.

"Gus missed a whole week of school already," Pete said. "At least with school closed, he won't get further behind."

Mom clicked off the radio. "Gus never has to worry about that. He's a good student." Was that why Dad had taken Gus? Because he could catch up in his lessons quicker?

"I wish your dad would call, just to say they're safe," Mom said. "I talked to Mr. Geswein next door, and he said not to worry, that they're probably helping with evacuations."

"If Dad doesn't come home before Sunday, how will we get to church? Dad has the car."

"There won't be Mass," Mom said. "Mr. Geswein said water came right up the front steps of Saint Joe's, and nobody could go to Mass without hip boots."

"We got any hip boots?" Pete asked.

Mom laughed. "God will forgive us this one Sunday."

"I didn't mean for church. They might come in handy if we need to go down to Wally's for something." *Or Richie's house,* he thought. If water was up to the front door of Saint Joe's on Third, how were Richie and his dad faring down on Second?

"I think your dad has a pair in the basement," Mom said. "Likely on a hook under the stairs."

Pete opened the basement door and flipped the switch for the bare lightbulb that hung from the basement ceiling.

The light dangled from its wire, swaying just a bit.

As he started down the steps, Pete saw reflections from the light bulb across the basement floor. The *wet* basement floor. It hadn't been wet when he'd stoked the furnace after school.

Pete hurried down the steps to look closer. The floor wasn't just wet. It was covered with two inches of water!

CHAPTER 13

FIREWOOD

Pete had worried about water in Richie's basement, never expecting it to happen here. On Fifth Street! He hurried upstairs and grabbed his boots from beside the sunroom door, where he'd left them after school. Stepping into them on the basement steps, he didn't bother to fasten them.

Calm down, he told himself. There could be more than one reason for water in the basement. Running his hands along the brick foundation, he felt the damp basement wall. The wall always felt *damp*, but no water oozed from the mortar between the bricks. This was more than seepage from the saturated ground.

Pete checked the plumbing for leaks and found none.

Only one explanation remained. This was floodwater! The Ohio River was in their basement!

Pete found Dad's hip boots under the stairs. He shoveled coal into the furnace and eyeballed the distance from the waterline to the furnace grate. Less than a foot of water and they'd have no heat. He added more coal to the furnace. Better get as much heat now as they could.

Upstairs, he put the hip boots in the coat closet and slipped his arms into the sleeves of his old jacket. The moonless sky drizzled rain down his collar as he hurried to the woodpile beside the garage. He lugged armload after armload of wood and tumbled it on the sunroom floor.

On his fourth trip, Mom stood in the kitchen doorway when he came in. "What in heaven's name are you doing?"

It took Pete a few seconds to catch his breath, while she waited with her hands on her hips.

"I'm bringing in wood to dry," he said, "so I can build a fire in the fireplace tomorrow."

She squinted at him. "Surely we're not low on coal. Your dad said there was plenty."

"Plenty of coal," Pete said, watching worry flood her eyes, "but there's a little water in the basement, and I just wanted to be ready. You know, just in case."

"You mean in case the furnace goes out?" The worry in her eyes spread to her mouth and even to her hands, which she nervously rubbed together. "How much water?"

"Just a little," he said, "nothing to fret over."

Mom grabbed the yardstick from inside the pantry and took it to the basement. Standing on the bottom step, she dipped it to the floor and held it up to where the light shined on it. "More than three inches," she said. "Enough to fret over."

Putting on her everyday coat, she joined Pete in carrying wood, until they covered the sunroom floor with soggy logs that dripped onto the painted floorboards.

Pete stepped back outside and brushed small flecks of bark from the front of his jacket. Mom hung up her wet coat and whisked rain from her hair with her fingertips.

"Maybe it won't get any deeper," Pete tried to assure her.

She blew out her breath in a loud *huff*. "And maybe the Angel Gabriel will drop in for breakfast."

He kissed her cheek. "Go to bed. I want to bring up a few things from the basement."

"I'll help," she said.

"Go on up. I can take care of it. I'll be up in a minute."

"Make sure the Christmas box is on a high shelf," she said. "Your dad knew what he was doing, Pete, leaving you here to take care of things."

Was she right? Was that why Dad had chosen Gus? Because he wanted Pete to take care of Mom and the kids and the house? Maybe Pete had been wrong about Dad.

CHAPTER 14

LIGHT AND LUCK

Standing in the basement in water that lapped over the toes of his boots, Pete tried to think clearly. This wasn't supposed to happen on Fifth Street. The river wasn't *allowed* to be this high. He had worried about Richie and Dad and Gus. He had planned to help folks on the riverfront. He had not planned for *this*.

Think, Pete, he told himself. *You need to handle this.* What should go upstairs? Richie's dad had taken up an old hotplate for cooking. There was nothing like that here. And surely the water wouldn't rise as high as *their* stove. Not on Fifth Street. But who knew what that blasted river would do?

Pete spotted a row of oil lamps on a shelf next to a gallon of lamp oil. Mom had used those lamps a couple times during spring thunderstorms, when the electricity had gone out. Could the water get high enough to take out the electric lines?

Pete's eyes followed the wires strung above the basement rafters. The only wire below the rafters was the one the

60

lightbulb hung from. No water could get that high. But how many times had he said that this week and been wrong?

He dragged the stepladder from its place against the wall, its legs leaving a small wake behind them. He opened the ladder beneath the bulb, and grabbed the broom Dad used for sweeping up coal dust. He pulled on the heavy, coal-shoveling gloves. Standing on the ladder, he lifted the broom and maneuvered it across the rafters, bracing it against floor joists a foot or so from the lightbulb.

Once the broom was secure, he held the hot bulb with his gloved hands and eased it up, draping its wire over the broom handle. Now it hung just a couple inches from the ceiling. An extra foot and a half above the water on the floor.

As Pete stepped from the ladder, he realized water was higher on his boots than when he'd come down to the basement. If Dad had left him here to take care of things, he'd better get to it. Making three trips, he lined up the lamps and oil on the table in the sunroom.

He found himself thinking about Dad. *What else should I take up, Dad?* Not the coal shovel. He'd still need it down here. Not his old sled that leaned against the brick foundation.

He scanned the shelves. He'd take up Mom's garden tools to keep them from rusting. Empty Mason jars could stay. He eased the box marked *Christmas*, the one with ornaments Mom had carefully wrapped, from the top shelf. He carried it up and slid it under a pantry shelf.

Another look around the basement revealed a small pile of bricks stacked beside the furnace. They'd been removed from the foundation when the coal chute was installed, back when Pete was little. He had tried to build a fort with them once, but there were too few to make much of anything. He put them in the pantry. Maybe they would prove useful yet.

Before he closed the pantry door, he opened the Christmas box and lifted out the Quaker Oats container filled with bottle-cap ornaments he and Gus had made. Sifting through them, he found the one marked *7-Up*. He remembered how Gus used to rub his thumb across the 7 for luck. Pete put the ornament in his pocket.

As he lay in bed, trying to figure out what else needed to be done, he talked to Dad again. *Did you ever imagine a flood in our basement? How high can it get down there? What should I do?* Before Dad had left, he'd said, "Don't let me down, Pete."

I'll try my best, Dad, he promised, as the rain continued to drum overhead. He reached over the side of his bed to where his trousers lay in a heap on the floor. Pulling the 7-Up bottle cap from the pocket, he rubbed his thumb across the 7.

We need some luck. Likely you and Gus need some, too.

CHAPTER 15

SNOW

Something woke Pete. Not a noise exactly. The clock on the dresser said two thirty. He listened hard, but he didn't hear anything. That was it! He didn't hear anything! No patter of rain on the roof or the windowpanes. The rain had stopped! Maybe, just maybe, he'd gotten his luck and the flood fears were over.

~~~

When Pete looked out the window in the early-morning light, he saw the rain *had* stopped during the night, but the backyard was covered in snow. Snow, for crying out loud! And flakes still tumbled from the sky.

Mom was in the kitchen, frying sausage in a skillet. Timmy sat on the sunroom floor, building a fence with the logs Pete and Mom had plunked there the night before. Etta sat at the picnic table, fiddling with one of the oil lamps.

"Don't play with that, Etta," Pete said.

"What's it for?" she asked.

"For light," Pete answered.

She squinted at the lamp's glass chimney. "Where does the lightbulb go?"

Pete ignored her and grabbed the hip boots before heading to the basement. He slid into them on the basement steps, where the kids couldn't see him and ask more questions.

Mom had left the yardstick leaning against the wall on the top step, and Pete carried it down with him. It dipped into the water more than eight inches, and came out wearing a coat of wet coal dust. Eight inches! How could this happen? On Fifth Street?

Pete shoveled dry coal from the top of the pile into the furnace, hoping the heat would last through the day. But water lapped close at the fire's heels. If it kept rising, the furnace would be snuffed out before noon.

Mom carried breakfast into the sunroom, a stern look on her face. "Who's been into the oatmeal cookies?" she asked. "Those were for Gus, and half of them are gone."

"Not me," Etta said. "Can we play in the snow?"

"We could build a snowman!" Timmy said.

"Not enough snow for that," Pete said. "It melts near as fast as it hits the wet ground." *And makes the river rise.* "You should stay inside and keep warm." Pete didn't know how much longer they'd have heat in the house.

"What about the cookies?" Mom asked again.

"What about the snow?" Etta asked.

Mom shrugged. "It won't hurt them to have a little fun.

They've been cooped up too long. I can bake more cookies later."

Pete understood. They were kids. But should he warn Mom about the furnace? He watched Timmy and Etta bundle into coats, scarves, and mittens. And said nothing.

Dad had expected Pete to take care of the house, but Dad hadn't planned on water in the basement. What would Dad want him to do now? It was as if Dad answered: *Prepare for the worst.*

"Can you help me with the rowboat?" Pete asked Mom.

"The rowboat?"

"I want to tie it to the front porch, but I can't move it there by myself."

"A rowboat on the front porch?" The tone in her voice and look on her face said she thought he'd lost his mind.

"Just beside it."

"In my flower bed?"

"I'll move it long before your bulbs even think about sprouting," he said.

The skeptical look stayed on her face, but she helped Pete drag the rowboat from the garage, while Timmy and Etta pelted them with questions.

"I just want to have it handy," Pete said as he tied the boat's tow rope to the porch rail. "In case we need it." *In case the worst happens.*

CHAPTER 16

TO THE STORE

Snow changed back to rain, and Pete built a fire in the fireplace. His mind was still in the garage. When they'd hauled out the rowboat, his eyes had caught sight of something in the corner. Black and resembling a bucket or metal lantern without chimney glass, Pete knew what it was. A coal oil stove! Dad sometimes used it to warm his hands when he and Pete worked in the garage on cold winter days.

Pete would fetch it inside after going to Wally's Corner Store to pick up a few supplies—and a bit of fresh news. The *Ironton Tribune* office was flooded and would print no more newspapers until the floodwater went down.

Pete's feet sloshed along the wet sidewalk, splashing with every step. At a cross street, one look toward the river showed rowboats moving along Fourth Street as though they were cars!

The flood was only a block from home, and the basement was filling with water! How could this happen? On low-lying Railroad Street, which ran down the center of town, muddy water nearly lapped over the top of Pete's boots. He had never imagined anything like this. He wanted to talk to Dad. But Dad and Gus had been gone for six days! Where were they?

Pete slipped off one glove and slid his hand in his pocket. He felt for the bottle-cap ornament and rubbed his thumb across its face. *For luck, Gus. For you and Dad. For all of us.*

With Fourth Street flooded, Wally's would be closed. Pete plodded several blocks along Fifth and up to Sixth before he found an open store. He was drenched when he stepped inside, dripping puddles on the floor as he walked to the counter.

The clerk was Mr. Dietz from Saint Joe's.

"You heard anything about the men who went to fill sandbags in the West End?" Pete asked.

"Water breached those sandbags days ago," the man said. "The men must've all gone home."

"My dad and brother haven't come home yet," Pete said, trying to keep the fear from his voice.

"They evacuated everyone from there," Mr. Dietz said. "Took folks to schools, the courthouse, and the post office. They even put families in cabooses in the rail yard. Look in those places."

Dad and Gus wouldn't have evacuated to one of those places. They would have come home. And Pete couldn't go to look for them anyway. His responsibility was home and Mom and the kids.

"You got any coal oil?" Pete asked. He bought as much as he could carry. And he bought Tootsie Rolls. Chewing on those would keep Etta and Timmy quiet for a while.

Mr. Dietz told him mail wasn't going to get through for the next few days. "And they're not selling gasoline anymore. Not until the flood goes down. They said folks are s'posed to get typhoid shots, but I'm not sure where."

"Typhoid?"

"You catch it from contaminated water. Like floodwater."

~~~

When Pete walked through the sunroom to the kitchen, Mom stirred vegetable soup at the stove. The steamy smell seemed to warm the room, and Pete took a deep sniff.

"Pete, I'm glad you're home." Mom's voice sounded worried. "The furnace quit."

"I figured as much," he said, deciding not to tell her how much the river had encroached or what Mr. Dietz had said about the West End. If Dad wanted Pete to take care of things, he'd take care of the worrying, too.

Pete went to the sunroom for firewood.

"Iva Taylor's heat is out, too," Mom said, "so I invited her here. She can't stay alone in that cold house. I'll make you up a bed on the couch tonight and put her in your room."

"Sleeping on the couch is perfect," he said. "I can keep the fire going all night."

He carried an armload of wood through the dining room and around the corner to the living room. The fire crackled, and Mrs. Taylor sat on the couch, her knitting needles catching firelight and flashing it around the room.

Her cat, Imogene, tried to pounce on the specks of light that glanced on the rug. As each disappeared from under her paws, the cat found another to tackle. She never seemed to tire of the game, and Timmy and Etta never tired of watching her.

Pete had forgotten about Imogene. Giving up his room to Mrs. Taylor was not a problem. But her creepy, weird-eyed cat? Pete sighed as he threw another log on the fire.

"I didn't want to put you out of your bed, Pete," Mrs. Taylor said, her knitting needles never slowing, "but your mother was quite insistent."

"I don't mind," Pete told her.

"Your mother doesn't realize how many floods I've lived through," the woman said. "I admit, this one is a little too big for its britches, but we'll weather it. Just like always."

A little too big for its britches? Pete thought about the things Mr. Dietz had reported. Pete might not have lived through a lot of floods, but he knew *this* was no ordinary flood.

CHAPTER 17

THE BICYCLE

Mr. Dietz had said folks were evacuated to the post office. That's where Dad worked. Likely Dad was helping there. But why hadn't he called?

Pulling the telephone around the newel-post, Pete sat on the small landing. He took a few deep breaths. He didn't want his voice to sound alarmed. *Dad's fine,* he told himself. And he tried really hard to believe it.

Pete knew Dad's work number by heart, so he'd call that line. He picked up the receiver, but the telephone was dead. How long had it been dead? No wonder Dad hadn't called.

They're at the post office, but they can't call. That's what Pete chose to believe. He had to believe they were all right, since he couldn't do anything to look for them anyway. His work was here.

Water in the basement had reached the third step, and almost swallowed the yardstick. Looking at the dirty water, the word *typhoid* seeped into Pete's mind. He had to keep the family safe. He hurried up the stairs and locked the basement door. He dropped the key into his pocket.

After bringing more firewood into the sunroom to dry, Pete went to the garage for the small coal oil stove. He looked around the garage to ferret out anything else that might prove useful. Dad's spare flashlight sat on the workbench at the rear of the garage. *What?* He looked again. The flashlight didn't belong here. Dad always kept it in the Buick. Why would he have left it *here?*

Pete touched the flashlight, still not quite believing it was real. Aunt Mary always said, *God provides.* But surely God didn't move the flashlight from the Buick. And what was God providing it for? Was Pete going to need it?

He grabbed the flashlight and the coal oil stove, and stepped out into the rain. Reaching to pull the door closed behind him, something else caught his eye. Not an object, but an empty space where something was missing. His bicycle!

It had been here on Wednesday when he patched the rowboat's leak, but what about earlier today when he and Mom had moved the boat? He wasn't sure.

Pete searched the garage. Gus's bike leaned against the garage wall, its rear tire flatter than a busted balloon. The old red wagon stood beside it. Only Pete's bicycle was missing. And it wasn't just any bicycle. Pete's Schwinn Streamline Aerocycle.

He remembered back to Wednesday. The night he'd been awakened by the bang of a door. The side door to the garage was never locked. Had someone come in and stolen his bike? Why would anyone do that? And who would have done it?

President Roosevelt had said a third of the nation was still suffering in poverty from the Depression. Was someone in Ironton so poor he'd stolen Pete's Schwinn? Pete would have gladly lent his bicycle if anyone needed it, but knowing someone had sneaked in and taken it sent shivers down his back. He jerked his head around, almost expecting someone to be creeping up behind him. He had to be more watchful, more careful.

As rain pattered on the shingled roof, Pete slid the bar on the main garage doors. He looked around again, even though he knew he was alone. He grabbed the side door key from its hook beside the light switch. He'd keep both doors locked from now on.

Dad expected Pete to handle things at home, but who knew the basement would flood, the heat would go out, and a bicycle thief would strike?

CHAPTER 18

ON
FIFTH
STREET

Pete nearly tripped over Imogene as he walked through the sunroom.

"Mom, did you lend my bicycle to somebody?" he asked as he pushed Imogene aside with his foot and walked into the kitchen. "Or move it somewhere?"

"Isn't it in the garage?"

He shook his head and plunked the flashlight and garage key on the windowsill above the stove.

"I haven't seen it." She pointed to the object in his hand. "Is that your dad's old coal oil stove?"

"If I can figure out how to get it working," he said, "you can use it upstairs tonight. I know the fireplace doesn't help much up there."

"I didn't know your dad still had that," she said, "and I doubt we have any coal oil."

"I bought some when I was at the store. Bought some Tootsie Rolls for the kids, too."

"Your dad will be proud of you." She kissed his forehead.

73

"Mommy! Mommy!" Etta ran into the kitchen, Timmy close on her heels. "There's water in our street!"

"Dirty water," Timmy added.

Mom and Pete rushed to the living room and stepped outside. Rain pounded the porch roof, the porch steps, and their front walk. Pete's eyes followed the walk to where it led down two more steps to the sidewalk. The sodden lawn sloped beside those steps, and rain ran from the grass and splashed down the steps like a waterfall. The Norway maple growing in the strip of grass between sidewalk and curb dipped its branches toward the street. But the street's bricks were hidden under floodwater.

"Good Lord, Pete!" Mom said. "Fifth Street is flooded!"

Timmy and Etta clung to Mom's skirt, their eyes wide.

Mom quickly regained control of herself and grabbed their hands. "We'll be safe and dry inside," she said.

"And warm," Pete added. "I just need to get the coal oil stove going. And after supper, Tootsie Rolls."

"Yay!" Etta said, and Timmy echoed her.

Mom told Pete to put the stove in her room, and she would move Etta and Timmy into bed with her. "We'll all be warmer that way," she said. "I'll give Iva plenty of wool blankets to use in your room. I can even fill a couple of hot water bottles for her. No flood will get the best of us."

When Pete had the stove functioning, he put the toolbox on the floor by the couch. He had a feeling he'd need it again.

The kids plopped down by the fire as Pete turned on the

radio, now the only source of news. With their Fourth Street offices underwater, *both* Ironton newspapers had shut down. Ironton radio station WCMI preempted regular shows to broadcast only flood news. WLW out of Cincinnati did the same.

"What about *Jack Armstrong, the All-American Boy?*" Etta asked. "They said tune in next time."

"*Next time* isn't until Monday," Pete said. "But I doubt it'll be on then either. Not until after the flood."

"But we won't know what happens!" Etta was distraught. "And what about *Little Orphan Annie?*"

"Leapin' Lizards!" Timmy used Annie's favorite expression. "I want *Orphan Annie.*" He stomped his foot.

The radio announcer interrupted the news to ask, "Has anyone sighted Thomas Spurlock? His family is worried about him."

"Why is the radio worried about Mr. Spurlock?" Etta asked. "Is he lost?"

"I don't know," Pete said, realizing Dad and Gus might not be the only ones unaccounted for. How many others were missing? And where were they?

CHAPTER 19

ROWBOATS

"What about Mr. Spurlock?" Etta asked again.

Timmy tugged on Pete's arm. "What about *'Merican Boy?*"

Pete had to distract them. "Mr. Spurlock is probably hiding from those seven kids of his. Wouldn't you hightail it from that crazy family?"

Etta sniffled. "Charley is crazy, but Alice is my friend."

"Tell you what," Pete said. "Find the last *Tribune* that came and I'll read *Katzenjammer Kids* to you and Timmy."

"Will you do the funny voices?" Etta asked.

"If you behave," Pete said. He dreaded the prospect of reading the same comic strip over and over for days until the *Trib* went back to work, but it would be worth it to keep the kids from being scared and cranky.

As Pete read the words, his mind was on Mr. Spurlock. Why was he missing? Was the man hurt? The Spurlocks lived down near Saint Joe's, which was now flooded. While

Pete had worried about water in the basement, what had the rest of Ironton dealt with?

Pete had tried so hard to believe Dad and Gus were safe at the post office, but doubts had niggled at his brain. Now those doubts grew into giant fears. His voice caught in the middle of a word, but Etta and Timmy seemed to think he was just being funny.

~~~

Mrs. Taylor's cat stretched out like an accordion before she curled up at the fireside. Pete pulled his blanket up as far as his nose and peeped out at the flames. They seemed alive as they crackled and chirped, providing company as well as heat. But they were no comfort. He had allowed the doubts to get inside, and they wouldn't leave him alone.

During the night, he got up and threw another log on the fire. He padded through the house and unlocked the basement door. He didn't need the yardstick to check the water level. Only four steps climbed from the murky depths. The lightbulb still hung above the water's reach, but it was clear to Pete the bulb would eventually lose the battle.

He clicked off the light switch and pushed Imogene out of the way to close the door. He turned the key in the lock and went to the fuse box in the front room's coat closet. It was eye level, and Dad had clearly marked the fuses. Pete unscrewed the fuse for the basement. When he closed the closet door, he barely missed Imogene's tail. *Stupid cat! Stop following me!*

He slumped back to the couch, but he couldn't sleep.

It was nearly dawn when Pete got up to throw another log into the fireplace. He heard voices from close by. Male voices. Dad and Gus? They were home? He nearly dropped a log on his toes.

He flung open the front door. Men were in the yard, but it wasn't Dad or Gus. And the voices didn't sound familiar. Pete squinted to see if he could tell what the men were up to.

Standing in the doorway, Pete tried to look intimidating, in case the men were no-accounts. He squinted to penetrate the darkness, but saw only shapes. Figures sat where the lawn sloped beside the two concrete steps leading down to the sidewalk. Why would men sit on wet ground?

Stepping onto the porch in his bare feet, ignoring the cold that seeped into his soles, Pete looked closer at the men. The black sky eased to gray as he looked toward the concrete steps. But he couldn't see those steps. Or the slope of lawn either. The Ohio River covered them!

Water surrounded the trunk of the Norway maple near the curb, and two rowboats were tied to it. Other rowboats floated at the edge of the yard. Rowboats with men aboard. Rowboats, for crying out loud! In the Brinkmeyer front yard! As if the house were a bait shop!

CHAPTER 20

IMOGENE

Pete went back inside for his shoes and coat before he went outside to talk to the men in the rowboats. Nearly tripping over Imogene, Pete eased out the front door, where water cascaded from the eaves to add to what fell from the sky.

Pete sloshed down the front walk. "What'cha doing here?" he called loud enough to be heard over the rain, which poured onto the rowboat men and splashed into the Fifth Street river. "At this hour?" he added, trying to make his voice sound deeper.

"River's been coming up pretty quick," one man said, as another cursed the flood with words that would knock Father Gloekner off his pulpit. Dad sometimes used similar words when he struggled to loosen a stubborn lug nut on the Buick's rims, but he always warned Pete not to talk like that.

"We been out looking for folks who need rescued or supplies brought to 'em," the first rowboat man said. "You need anything?"

"You want us to take you to a shelter?" another man asked.

The crude man swore again. "Water's so dad-blamed high, we had to duck under traffic lights when we rowed under 'em." He went on to describe the river with several more unsavory words.

"Hey!" Mom's voice yelled from the front porch. "I have young children upstairs, and I'll thank you to mind your language." She jabbed her finger toward the men in the yard.

"Jeez," the man at fault mumbled. "Sorry, ma'am. We're just trying to help."

"They came to see if we need supplies or want them to take us to a shelter," Pete told Mom.

"No," Mom said. "No shelter. We'll stay here until Dad and Gus come home. Otherwise, they won't know where to find us."

"Just a minute," Pete told the men. He went to the front porch and leaned in to Mom. "They could take Mrs. Taylor and Imogene."

~~~

"How nice of them," Mrs. Taylor said when Pete told her of the men's offer. "What do you think, Imogene? We could stay with Norma Lutz up on Ninth. She might be glad for the company. Some folks panic when the river rises. Us old-timers have more sense."

A man held an umbrella over Mrs. Taylor, as she hobbled down the watery sidewalk to his boat. Pete sloshed along beside her, carrying her knitting bag, satchel, pocketbook—and Imogene. When Mrs. Taylor was settled on the rowboat's seat, Pete handed her bags to one of the men.

Pete held out Imogene to Mrs. Taylor, but the cat dug her claws into his coat and wouldn't let go.

"Imogene doesn't care for rain," Mrs. Taylor explained.

Pete climbed into the boat to hand the cat to the woman. Apparently, Imogene didn't like the rocking of the boat either. Twice she hissed, screeched, and jumped back into Pete's arms.

"Hold her tighter," he told Mrs. Taylor. *Stupid cat!*

Firmly gripping her caterwauling pet, Mrs. Taylor looked to where Mom stood on the porch. "Take care of your mother, Pete. She tries to hide it, but she worries. I hope your father comes home soon."

Pete gave her a weak smile. "Me, too."

Don't let me down, Dad had said. Pete considered it a sacred trust. He had to take care of Mom and the kids.

~~~

While the kids played in the living room, Pete tried to convince Mom to evacuate. "At least think about it," he said.

"We'll leave when your father tells us to," she said. "Not a minute sooner."

Pete hoped she wasn't making a mistake. Mrs. Taylor said Mom was worried. Did Mom ever worry Dad might *not* come home? No! Pete couldn't even think about that possibility.

CHAPTER 21

PHOTOGRAPHS

Mom read stories to the kids all morning, while Pete worked in the pantry. He moved jars of canned food to the highest shelves. He moved sacks of flour and sugar. He couldn't defy Mom, but he had to safeguard everything he could.

Mom's Christmas box peeked out from beneath a bottom shelf. Maybe Pete could use it to make his point. He picked up the box and carried it through the living room.

"Where are you taking that?" Mom asked.

"Upstairs closet," he answered, "where it'll stay dry."

When he came back downstairs, Mom was holding the framed family photograph from beside the mantel clock. She ran her finger across Gus's face. And Dad's.

"I believe this is what he'd want us to do, Pete. I have to believe it." He noticed the firm set to her jaw, even though her chin quivered a bit.

"Show us the picture," Etta squealed.

Mom pasted a smile on her face and held the picture at

82

eye level for the kids. Timmy pointed to each person and named them. "Mommy, Daddy, Pete, Gus, Etta. Where's me?" he asked.

"See that baby in my arms?" Mom said. "That's you."

"But I'm not a baby," Timmy whined.

"Of course, you're not," Mom said. "After lunch, we'll get out the photograph album and find other pictures."

~~~

Pete looked over Mom's shoulder, and photographs flooded his mind with memories. Standing beside Gus in the snowy front yard with their sled. His First Communion photo with him and Richie both looking choked in matching stiff collars. A Halloween picture of him, Gus, and Richie dressed as the Three Musketeers. Pete reached into his pocket and felt for the bottle cap he now carried everywhere with him.

Come on, luck, he said to himself. *The other Musketeers need you.*

~~~

That night, the radio reported Hudson-Pillar Hardware at Second and Lawrence had caught fire and burned to the waterline. Someone reported seeing a house float away along the riverfront. The river was predicted to rise another two feet before it crested. Pete blew out his breath.

The announcer requested listeners to pray for the rain to stop. While hymns played, radio voices went silent to allow for the prayers. Mom and Pete prayed, not only for the rain to stop, but for Gus and Dad, for Richie Weber's family, and for everyone in town. Pete couldn't remember ever meaning his prayers more than that night. He added a silent prayer that the foundation of their house was stable enough to withstand the flood's onslaught.

And he did more than pray. Was it a sin to question God? Because Pete had a whole string of questions. Hadn't folks suffered enough through the Depression? Wasn't someone stealing Pete's bicycle enough? Wasn't the endless rain enough? Now the angry river had flooded Fifth Street and taken over their basement. *Are you testing us, God? You know I don't like tests.*

"I forgot to change the sheets in your room after Iva Taylor left," Mom broke into his thoughts and clicked off the radio. "My mind just isn't where it's supposed to be."

He patted her shoulder. "The flood has us all on edge. Don't worry about the sheets. I'll stay on the couch and keep an eye on the fire." *And on the water in the basement.*

"You understand why we need to stay, don't you, Pete?"

"No, I don't," he said. "But I'll stay wherever you and the kids are." His thumb felt in his pocket for the bottle cap.

CHAPTER 22

PREPARING

Pete gave Mom enough time to fall asleep before he unlocked the basement door and peered in. Only the top step was visible above the waterline. He locked the door again. But no locked door could hold back a flood destined to rise.

Rain spat at the windows in defiance. Nothing on the first floor was safe. Pete felt sure of it.

He stoked the fire before making the first of what was to be many trips up the stairs. He carried up the brass clock from the mantel and put it on his dresser. He took up every can of coal oil he'd bought to feed the little stove in Mom's bedroom. He emptied the bookshelf and the newspaper rack. He lifted the prized photograph album that held his childhood memories and school days with Richie. Where was Richie now?

He removed the last of the books from the shelf and stacked them. As he was about to pick up the pile, something behind the bookshelf caught his eye. He wedged his hand between the shelf and the wall until his fingers latched onto another book. Gus's Shakespeare book! What was it doing there? He added the book to his stack.

As Pete lugged the books up the steps, Gus's book slid off the top. He lunged to catch it between his hip and the stair rail, so it wouldn't crash to the floor and wake Mom and the kids. He managed to snag the book, but a few papers slid from between its pages.

When he retrieved the dropped papers, the light from the top of the stairs revealed Gus's handwriting. Pete slid the papers into the book and tried to shove Gus to the back of his mind.

"I can't think about Gus," he murmured, trudging up the stairs with another armload. But Gus's face stared at him from the mantel photograph he carried. Dad's face was there, too. Maybe Dad and Gus were on their way home. Pete had to do what Dad expected of him. He almost felt the river lapping at his heels as he kept moving.

Don't think about Dad. Just work. Pete made more trips. A dishpan full of cups and plates. The hand-painted cookie tin. The oil lamps. Electric lamps. All eight dining room chairs. He put half in his room and the others in the kids' empty front bedroom.

The living room rocker was the toughest struggle. Not only was it heavy, but its size made it awkward to carry. But Pete was determined. He managed to get it up the steps without banging its rockers against the banister's spindles.

He even rolled up the living room rug, dragged it into the dining room, and laid it across the table. Surely, the water couldn't reach it there.

He filled every empty jug in the pantry with clean tap water and set them on the highest shelves beside the food he'd already moved there. He draped the curtains over the curtain rods and took the yardstick to the top of the stairs. He unplugged the radio from the wall outlet and lugged it up the steps.

It was late, and his arms and back ached. He threw a log on the fire and plopped on the couch. For only a minute. Just long enough to catch his breath. Because there was still more to do. Maybe he'd close his eyes for a few seconds. No more than that.

But when his eyes flew open, he knew it was nearly dawn. The fire's glow shined on the bare wood where the rug had been. What was that in the middle of the floor?

He jumped up to get a better look. A bubble. Seeping through the floorboards. The mighty Ohio was coming through the floor!

CHAPTER 23

MOVING UPSTAIRS

N ow the river truly *was* at his heels. And a voice inside his head said *Hurry! Hurry!* Pete carried the toolbox to the kitchen. He unplugged the refrigerator from the wall. Steadying his shaking hands, he used a pair of Channellocks to disconnect the Kelvinator's motor and wrapped it in an old towel. He carried it up to his room and lifted it to the shelf in his closet. He was glad Dad had taught him about tools.

Can't think about Dad now. Hurry!

Scanning the kitchen one last time, Pete grabbed Dad's spare flashlight from the windowsill, the flashlight God had provided. He flipped the kitchen light switch to the *off* position before doing the same in the dining room.

At the fuse box in the coat closet, he unscrewed the fuses for the first-floor outlets and plunked them in his pocket. If water reached the first floor's wiring, it wouldn't short out the whole house. The wires from the street were high enough on the house to keep the electricity on. Surely, *surely*, the water wouldn't reach the second floor.

Before Pete closed the closet door, he grabbed winter coats and scarves and flung them over the banister. *Hurry!*

By the beam of the flashlight, he groped his way through the kitchen and propped open the pantry door with the iron doorstop. He'd need to get in there later, floodwater or not.

The pile of bricks he'd brought up from the basement sat on the floor inside the pantry. He hauled them to the living room and stacked them. Two bricks. Four bricks. He managed to get them six-high under each of the couch's legs. *Hurry!*

Pete heard Mom in her room overhead, as dawn struggled to ease the kitchen's darkness. With the hip boots draped across his arm, he grabbed a bottle of milk and some hardboiled eggs from the dark refrigerator. His shoes splashed through a spreading puddle on the living room floor.

The toilet flushed. Timmy's feet pattered down the hall.

"Pete!" Mom called. "What's all this stuff doing up here?"

"Just stay there," Pete said. "I'm bringing up breakfast." He had to keep her calm, keep the kids calm. Keep himself calm.

~~~

"Your room is our new living room," Pete told the kids.

"Why?" Etta asked.

89

"Because," Pete answered.

"It's too small," she complained.

Pete shoved Etta's and Timmy's beds against the wall.

"I'm cold," Etta said.

Pete handed Etta her winter coat and mittens. He set dining room chairs around the coal oil stove. He plugged in the radio.

Etta still wasn't happy. "Can you cut out paper ladies for me?" she asked.

Pete rummaged through the stack of newspapers and magazines he'd brought upstairs and found the Sears, Roebuck and Co. catalogue.

He went to his room for a pair of scissors. Scissors in hand, he noticed the book he'd set on his dresser the night before. Papers still protruded from its pages. Those pages with Gus's handwriting on them. He wanted to stop and read them, but Etta's voice whined from the front room.

Mom took the scissors and cut out pictures Etta selected from the women's clothing section of the catalogue. Etta danced the ladies in her mittened hands, as Timmy flipped through the catalogue's pages to find something for him.

"See if you can find a picture of a life preserver," Pete said. "We're gonna need it."

"That's enough," Mom said, giving Pete a warning look.

Why was she so stubborn? Didn't she realize how much danger they were in?

CHAPTER 24

LOVE POEM

Pete went to his room and snatched the papers from Gus's Shakespeare book. Gus's favorite book. The book hidden behind the bookshelf. Words in Gus's handwriting crawled across a paper, and markings like Morse code stood out at the top. *Dot-dash, dot-dash, dot-dash.* If it was Morse code, it was the letter *A* over and over. That didn't make sense.

Pete read the first line of words and realized the markings were not Morse code. Gus had called them *scansion.* Sister Ignatius had taught him to use those symbols to check meter when he wrote poems. This paper was the beginning of a poem.

> *Inside my heart, my blood pumps true*
> *With everlasting love for you.*
> *It thumps the rhythm of your name*
> *And "Venus, Venus" doth proclaim.*

Everlasting love? Doth proclaim? What kind of word was "doth?" Gus was writing a love poem to Venus Marlowe! *Ick!*

No wonder Gus had hidden the book. Pete knew he was never supposed to see this. How he wished he hadn't. He tried to erase the syrupy words from his brain. This was a side of Gus he didn't need to know. Didn't want to. Gus obviously hadn't stopped thinking about Venus, no matter what Mom and Dad had said. The poor sap was definitely stuck on her.

That explained why Gus had been angry when Mom and Dad had forbidden him to see Venus again. And he'd taken out his anger on Pete. Pete almost pitied Gus. Poor lovesick sap.

Pete wanted to tell Gus he was sorry, but he hadn't seen Gus in two weeks. And his last words with his brother had been angry ones. Had they been the last words *ever*? A feeling like an icy, wet hand reached inside him, sending chills up his back and arms. He rubbed his hands up and down his sleeves, but the shiver wouldn't let go.

Stop thinking about Gus. Take care of Mom and the kids, he told himself for the umpteenth time. *Dad is depending on you.*

~~~

At noontime, Pete pulled on the hip boots to go to the pantry for bread and pickles. The water on the first floor reached halfway to the knees of his hip boots, which stretched almost to his armpits, like rubber overalls. He could feel the river's chill right through the heavy rubber.

Water crept up the legs of the dining room table. And rain still pattered against the windows. How much higher could it go? Would all his work be for nothing? Even up on bricks, the couch would be ruined. But the stove and refrigerator could be cleaned and most everything else had been moved upstairs. Pete had done all he could. Hadn't he? Would it be enough?

Slogging through the kitchen, dining room, and living room with his hands full of food was difficult. The weight of the heavy boots and force of the water against his legs slowed him, threatened to knock him over.

He took up enough food for supper, too, not knowing how high the water would rise in another few hours.

"I don't know how much longer I'll be able to get things from the pantry," he told Mom as he lined up food jars on the dresser.

He waited for Mom to comment, but she sat stoically in the rocker. What did she expect him to do? What about tomorrow? What would happen if the river rose to the second floor? Would they have to climb to the roof? Could they?

CHAPTER 25

WAITING

Pete and Mom listened to the radio. It reported the Water Works Pumping Station had more than two feet of water and was out of service.

"I put jugs of clean water on the pantry shelf," Pete said. "I'll bring them up before the water gets too deep. And I can fill a bucket with river water for flushing the toilet." He laughed a hollow laugh. "That's one thing we have plenty of." It was about time the river served a useful purpose.

There seemed to be no end to the radio's bad news. The James Moore Building at Second and Center Streets had collapsed that morning. The watchman on duty had narrowly escaped and been saved by rescue boats. The building had housed the liquor store where Richie Weber's dad worked. And the American Legion hall.

Mom's face looked ready to crumple.

"Mr. Dietz at the market said they evacuated everybody from down there last week," Pete reminded her.

"I know," she said, regaining her composure. "We just

have to wait a little longer. They'll be home any minute."

"How?" Pete asked. "By boat? They're probably looking for us in shelters."

"We'll wait here," she said firmly.

~~~

Tuesday began like Monday. Pete went to the top of the stairs to see how far the river had risen during the night. It covered the landing, where the stairs turned to go down two more steps. He reached through the stairway spindles with the yardstick. Twenty-six inches deep! In their living room! The river had declared war. And was winning every battle.

After breakfast—hardboiled eggs again—Pete read *Little Orphan Annie* to the kids for the hundredth time. Etta knew the lines by heart and said them before Pete got to them.

"If you know it, why do you need me to read it?" he asked.

"Cuz you can do the voices. You make Daddy Warbucks sound like the Daddy Warbucks on the radio."

Pete's laugh rang out like church bells at Christmas. And something amazing happened—the rain stopped! Sun came out from behind clouds that had seemed permanently glued to the skies above Ironton.

After nearly a month of gray days, sunlight streamed through windowpanes like a heavenly beacon. It was almost blinding, and Pete turned off the electric lamp.

"Hurray!" Timmy cheered.

"You said when the flood was over, we could listen to

Jack Armstrong, the All-American Boy," Etta said.

"The rain may have stopped," Pete said, "but we're still in a flood." *And who knows when the rain might start again.*

Wearing hip boots, Pete went to check on the first floor. Water was over his knees, and walking was slow and labored.

Back upstairs, he told Mom, "With the rain stopped, it's a good time to evacuate. I don't know how many more times I can go downstairs. The water's still rising."

"But the rain stopped," Etta said.

"There's still a lot of runoff to make it go higher," Pete said. "And who knows how much more snow is melting upriver to add to it. Hard to tell when it'll crest."

"Let's see what the radio says about it," Mom said.

The announcer's words were punctuated by the crackle of static, but estimates varied from six more inches to three more feet before the river would crest. Another brick building had collapsed on Second Street. No one was believed to be inside at the time. How much water did it take to collapse a building? How much would it take to collapse their house on Fifth Street?

CHAPTER 26

A DECISION

Pete leaned closer to the radio to see if they told *which* building had collapsed and *where* on Second Street. He hadn't heard from Richie in over a week. A report on property damage began, but static interrupted.

"Great God in heaven!" Pete yelled. "That's enough."

As if God answered, the noise quit. So did the announcer's voice. The radio was dead. Pete flipped the light switch. Nothing. The electricity was off.

Pete reached out his raised palms. "Now can we evacuate?"

"There's sunlight," Mom said. "Flashlight and oil lamps for after dark."

"And the Ohio River rising in our living room," Pete said, his voice rising, too. "We need to evacuate."

"What's *'vacuate*?" Timmy asked.

"Not without Dad and Gus," Mom said. "How will they find us? And I don't want the children in a shelter with strangers."

"What about Aunt Mary's?" Pete asked. "The river will never get as high as her place." Not long ago, he'd said the same thing about their house on Fifth Street. "With telephones out, we ought to check on Aunt Mary anyway. We can leave Dad a note."

Mom shook her head. "He'd expect us to stay."

But Pete was determined. "Dad trusted me to know best. If I decide it's best to evacuate, that's what we should do."

Timmy stomped his foot. "What's *'vacuate*?"

"It means going someplace else," Pete said.

"Someplace warm?" Etta asked, her teeth chattering, her hands tucked inside the sleeves of her winter coat.

Mom pulled Etta onto her lap. They rocked in the rocking chair, Mom's arms around Etta, her mouth a firm, straight line.

"Pete thinks he's boss," Etta said. "But you're the boss, right, Mom?"

Pete said nothing. He went down the hall to the window at the top of the stairs. Muddy water washed against the house, climbing the windows of the sunroom. Even if the river rose three more feet, it wouldn't quite reach the second floor. But how much water would it take to knock the house off its brick foundation?

Frustrated, Pete went into the bathroom. Opening a jug of clean water, he splashed some on his face. How could he convince Mom to evacuate? She was immovable when she dug in her heels.

He went back to the front room, where Mom spread jelly on a cracker for Timmy.

Pete's eyes darted around the room. "Where's Etta?"

"In the bathroom."

"No," Pete said. "I was just in there." The icy hand inside him went for his throat, and Pete bolted to the stairs.

Etta stood on the landing, knee-deep in floodwater! She let go of the banister, and the river snatched her up, trying to pull her deeper. Pete saw fear in her eyes as he bounded down the steps and scooped her up in his arms. Mom was on his heels.

As he turned to carry Etta upstairs to the hall, she cried, "My paper ladies. Save my paper ladies."

Mom leaned over the banister. "They're floating in my gravy boat." The fear had traveled from Etta's face to Mom's.

"It's a boat ride," Etta said, all fear cast aside.

Pete grabbed her by the shoulders and scolded, "You could have drowned. Stay away from the water! It's dangerous."

"I only have to do what Mom says," Etta replied. "Not you."

Mom put her hands on her hips and said, "Mom says you have to do what Pete says, too."

Etta's chin quivered, and Mom grabbed her in a hug. "Pete knows what's best for us," she said.

"But I think it's best to evacuate," Pete insisted.

Mom grimaced even as she nodded. "I'll help Etta change into dry clothes first."

CHAPTER 27

EVACUATING

Pete put on hip boots and eased down the steps. Moving from the landing into the first floor's depths, he fought off the image of Etta standing here not long ago. Even *he* had to tread carefully to keep water from sloshing over the top of the waders.

From the front window, he saw the rowboat still tied to the porch post, but instead of sitting in Mom's flower bed, it floated in what was now part of the Ohio River. Pete struggled to open the front door against the wall of water in the room. He left it open behind him and stepped into the river. On the porch!

Wanting to tug the boat as close as he could, he couldn't wedge it between the posts supporting the porch roof. He squeezed around it to push from behind, but he couldn't plant his feet securely because of the deep water.

The water won the tussle, seeping over the top of the hip boots. It soaked through his trousers as the river clutched him in its grasp and threatened to wash him away. The water on the porch was muddy, but it had seemed almost tame. Away from the porch, Pete felt its force.

He grabbed the stern of the boat and clung to it. He hadn't expected the river to be so strong. He pulled himself back to the porch. Catching his breath, he tightened the tow rope securing the rowboat and checked the leak he'd patched. It held.

Gripping the top of the porch rail, barely visible above the swollen Ohio, Pete managed to get inside to where Mom and the kids waited on the steps. He'd insisted on evacuating, but doubts swirled around inside his head. Maybe it was safer to stay here.

"Are we gonna drown?" Etta asked, her voice trembling.

"Of course not," Pete said. Did he sound sure?

Timmy seemed excited by this new adventure. "We're not scared, are we, Pete?" Pete was glad his little brother had no sense of the danger. Pete wished *he* were as confident.

The added water in the hip boots made it harder to move, so Pete dumped the water and put them back on. Changing into warm, dry clothes would have been welcome, but he wanted to get the family to Aunt Mary's before dusk.

He took Etta first, letting her cling to his back. "It's a piggyback ride," he told her. "Wrap your feet tight around me and don't let go." He heard her whimpering in his ear as they churned through the living room's depths and onto the porch. She gripped him tighter as he cautiously crossed the porch to the boat.

"I didn't mean it about you not being the boss," she said.

"I know."

After depositing Etta in the stern of the boat, Pete warned her, "Sit still."

He went back for Timmy. "Come on, Tim," he said. "Ready for your piggyback ride?"

With Timmy beside Etta in the boat, Pete instructed, "Wait here until I get back with Mom. Then we'll go for a boat ride."

"I'm cold," Etta said, shivering.

Pete shivered too, but he didn't say so. As he slogged through the living room's water, he asked Mom to grab a blanket from upstairs. From the porch, he tossed the blanket to Etta.

She stood to reach for it, and the boat wobbled.

"No standing in a boat," Pete yelled. "Sit still."

Etta dropped to the seat, and sat still as a tombstone. She didn't even touch the blanket, which lay in a mound at her feet.

Pete softened his voice. "I'll get Mom and be back in a minute. Just stay put."

But Mom was wary. "I don't think piggyback will work with me. I watched how you struggled through the water with the little ones. I'm too big for you to carry."

"You have to," Pete said. "There's no other way." But even as he said it, he thought of a way.

Mom followed him upstairs, where he raised a window

102

in her front bedroom. "You think you can slide down the porch roof? It's less than two feet from the edge of the roof to the rowboat."

Mom squinted out the window and bit her lip.

"The kids are waiting in the boat," he told her. "It's the roof or piggyback. You can't stay here alone."

She gave one affirmative jerk of her head. "Let's do it."

"I'll go first," he told her. "Then you slide down the roof and I'll help you into the boat."

The movement of her head was less firm, but she agreed.

Pete eased down the shingles of the porch roof. He dropped into the boat, causing it to rock wildly, tipping almost to the surface of the water.

Etta screamed and Timmy clutched the seat beneath him.

Trying to calm his racing heart, Pete braced his hip-booted feet on opposite sides of the boat and gradually steadied it.

"You said no standing," Etta scolded.

He ignored her. "All right, Mom," he called. "Ready?"

Mom slid down the roof on her rear, and turned to slide off the edge. Pete grasped her around the waist and helped her down to the boat. Again, he managed to steady the boat with his feet.

With Mom settled on the bow seat, Timmy stood to go to her.

"What did I say about no standing in a boat?" Pete

yelled. "I'm the captain. You have to mind me."

Timmy saluted and sat down. Pete wrapped the blanket around the two kids.

"Pete thinks he's *Jack Armstrong, the A-a-all-American Boy*," Etta said, stretching out the word *all* the way the man on the radio always did.

Pete untied the tow rope and settled onto the oarsman seat. He slid the oars into their locks. "I doubt Jack Armstrong ever had to row a boat right down the middle of Fifth Street. I never thought *I* would."

But even before they rowed away from the porch, doubts filled Pete's head. He felt the current grip the boat and struggled to row against its pull. He had never rowed in a flood before. Maybe evacuating was a mistake.

CHAPTER 28

OUT
OF THE
RIVER

Pete hoped he'd made the right decision. Had he taken his family from the uncertainty of their flooded home to the even-more-fickle whims of the expanding Ohio? The open bedroom window resembled a mouth caught in a scream. Pete fought back his own scream, along with a questioning lump in his throat.

But there was no going back. Lifting the kids from the boat would be more of a struggle than getting them here had been.

"Are we going for a boat ride or not?" Etta asked.

"You promised," Timmy said.

I have to do this, Pete told himself.

"Hey, Brinkmeyers!" Mr. Geswein called, poking his head out his upstairs window. "Try to keep your boat over the streets, so you won't snag on a lamppost or something."

Dangers Pete hadn't even thought of. "Are you going to evacuate?" he yelled to his neighbor.

"No, we'll stick it out now that the rain's stopped."

Should we have stuck it out, too? Pete wondered. *No,* he told himself. *Gesweins don't have young children to worry about.*

"If Dad or Gus comes looking for us, tell 'em we went to Aunt Mary's," Pete called. He braced his feet and plied the oars through the river in their front yard.

Rowing past the Norway maple's scraggly branches, Pete attempted to row down Fifth Street. But the unpredictable current tugged the boat in the wrong direction, and with street signs underwater, half-submerged houses were his only guideposts. At least it wasn't raining.

Inside the hip boots, the damp cold pierced Pete to his core. With each stroke of the oars, his bent knees tensed and tightened, straining against the thick rubber. An occasional sharp dig in his thigh told him the lucky bottle cap in his pocket was imprinting its jagged edges into his flesh.

The treacherous Ohio teemed with debris. Pete dipped the oars again and again, trying not to let the strain show on his face as he navigated around floating objects, from tires to teacups, following the unseen streets of watery Ironton.

"Look." Etta pointed. "Somebody's umbrella. I guess they don't need it since the rain stopped."

"Don't touch it!" Mom said. "Don't touch anything in this filthy water."

Pete rowed the boat to where he reasoned Walnut Street was, and tried to head up to Sixth. But he had to wrestle the oars to maneuver the boat. He gritted his teeth and pulled.

"Your face is red," Etta said.

Pete kept quiet and continued the struggle.

When the boat finally headed along Walnut to Sixth, the current lessened, but Pete didn't ease up. He knew the river's strength. After they crossed where Pete figured Sixth Street was, the oar brushed something beneath the water. Pete slipped the oar from its oarlock and tapped it on an underwater object.

"I think it's a fire hydrant," he said. "That means it's not as deep here."

Halfway to Seventh Street, he dipped the oar into the water again. It reached the bottom with most of the oar still showing.

"Dry land is close," Pete said. "Just a few more strokes."

"Hooray!" Timmy said.

When the boat's underbelly scraped the street, Pete climbed over the side. He tugged the tow rope and dragged the boat's weight to where rowboats lined the curb like parked cars on a day of store specials. Pete remembered when their yard on Fifth Street had looked this way, but that had been many feet of river water ago. At least the sidewalks weren't flooded here. Yet.

Adding their rowboat to the multitude, Pete lifted Mom over the shallow water in Seventh Street to a sidewalk above the river's clutches. She extended her arms for each of the kids. Etta and Timmy gripped Mom around the neck and hung on as tight as green apples. Mom's face finally softened its panicked look.

Mom held the kids' hands and marched toward Aunt Mary's.

When Aunt Mary opened her door, a streak of fur hurtled through the doorway and clawed at Pete's hip boots. Imogene! What was that dang cat doing here?

Pete carried the cat inside, where Mrs. Taylor sat on Aunt Mary's couch, her knitting needles flying. But it wasn't just Mrs. Taylor. The room was crammed full of people. Mom's sister, Aunt Maggie, with Uncle Mac and all the Hoffman cousins. And all seven Spurlock children from down by Saint Joe's.

Everyone seemed to talk at once.

"Imogene don't like our dog, Scruffy," Sally Hoffman said.

"Norma wasn't home," Mrs. Taylor put in. "Mary was nice enough to invite me here."

"Our daddy's name was called out on the radio," Alice Spurlock said.

"We heard it," Etta said. "Did you find him?"

As if in answer, Mr. and Mrs. Spurlock walked into the room. Mrs. Spurlock smiled. "Tom went upriver to help my brother check his livestock." Her smile quickly drooped. "Neither of them bothered to tell me they were going. I was sick with worry."

Mr. Spurlock patted her hand. "When I heard my name on the radio, I knew I'd better get on home or face the music."

The beginnings of an idea sprouted in Pete's head.

CHAPTER 29

KINGSBURY SCHOOL

He tugged off the hip boots, and someone handed him dry clothes. In the crowded room, he wasn't sure who. Judging by the old-fashioned look of them, they belonged to Uncle Mac or maybe even Aunt Mary's husband, who'd died in the flu epidemic of 1918.

In the bathroom, Pete unfolded the clothes to see . . . *knickers*! Knickers, for crying out loud! Nobody wore those short trousers anymore. But it felt good to wriggle out of cold, wet clothes and have something dry against his skin. He transferred the lucky bottle cap to the pocket of the knickers. Had the bottle cap been lucky? *They* were out of the river, but what about Dad and Gus?

Pete set his sodden oxfords on a sunny windowsill to dry, and traipsed around in his socks. With the crowd of feet in Aunt Mary's house, he had to be careful not to get his vulnerable toes stepped on.

Aunt Mary provided soup for supper. Its thin broth led Pete to suspect it had been watered down considerably when his family showed up. But he didn't care. Each swallow seemed to spread warmth into his arms and legs and clean to his fingers and toes.

When an orange glow faded to dark and brought an end to that first sunlit day, Aunt Mary assigned places for folks to bed down. Etta slept sideways in a bed with the Spurlock sisters and the Hoffman girls. Six in one bed!

Mrs. Taylor and Mrs. Spurlock shared a bed, while Aunt Maggie climbed in beside Aunt Mary. Mom and Timmy curled up on the sofa, and Uncle Mac and Mr. Spurlock slept sitting in chairs. All the young boys and Pete spread out on the floor.

It wasn't just the hard floor—or Imogene's curling up beside him—that kept Pete awake. His mind churned like the river. He was safe now. So were Mom and the kids. But how could he sleep comfortably with Dad and Gus still missing?

He had to do something. If Mr. Spurlock heard his name on the radio and came home, Pete had to tell the radio announcers about Dad and Gus.

~~~

In the morning, the entire full-to-the-rafters household ate canned peaches for breakfast. One of Aunt Mary's sweet-as-honey coffee cakes would have been too much for Pete to hope for.

The Hoffmans' mutt, Scruffy, and Imogene faced off like

sworn enemies, scuffling over food and water Aunt Mary put down for them.

"Imogene don't know how to share," Sally Hoffman said.

"Maybe Scruffy's the one who won't share," Etta defended.

Imogene took her complaints to Pete, sitting at his feet, yowling like a baby in a wet diaper. Pete tried to walk away, but walking away wasn't easy in a house jam-packed with people. And Imogene seemed tied to Pete's ankles.

"At noon, y'all need to go to Kingsbury Elementary to eat," Aunt Mary announced. "They have free milk, bread, and soup there. I can't feed twenty people, a dog, and a cat three meals a day. This isn't like the loaves and fishes in the Bible."

~~~

Lined up like army troops, the Brinkmeyers, Hoffmans, and Spurlocks marched toward Sixth Street's Kingsbury School. They walked the six blocks to Railroad Street before they had to get into rowboats to go further. Etta looked doubtful.

Pete rowed one of the boats. He'd almost forgotten the current's strength. At Sixth Street, he tried to keep the boat advancing straight ahead, but the river pushed it clean up to Seventh, where they found a dry place to get out.

While much of Sixth Street was underwater, Kingsbury's end of the street was higher ground, and the school sat on a rise.

Inside, long lines of people snaked through the corridor, waiting for free food. A peek into a classroom showed dozens of cots set up for residents whose homes were flooded. Another room was a makeshift hospital. *At least we don't need that,* Pete thought. *Mom was right to not bring the little ones here to stay.*

Aunt Mary's was crowded, but no one there was a stranger. Pete didn't recognize many of the faces in the endless line, and a few stared at his ill-fitting, out-of-date clothes.

"You look like you got dressed in 1915, Pete," said a voice from behind him.

Pete turned and looked into the face of Richie Weber's dad. Alive and well!

"You and Richie all right?" Pete asked. "I haven't heard from him since the first day he missed school."

"We're fine," Mr. Weber said. "He told me your idea to take the boat up and down the banks to see if folks need supplies or rescued. We been taking turns doing that every day."

So Richie and his dad had embarked on Pete's plan without him. Pete dismissed a twinge of missing out. He knew he'd been needed at home. And hearing that Richie was all right was like a miracle. *Thank God! But if you're not out of miracles yet, God, help us find Dad and Gus.*

CHAPTER 30
A MISSION

"You keeping dry at your place?" Mr. Weber asked. "Or are you staying here?"

"We're making do," Pete answered. "We moved up to Aunt Mary's yesterday. Where are you and Richie staying?"

"Been sleeping in a room over the Five and Dime. Water's in the first floor there, but we climb out the window and use our rowboat. Making do ain't new for us. Neither are bread lines."

Pete hadn't realized the Webers had been part of those lines that had sprung up during the Depression, even though he'd known those days had drained them. What would they do now with the liquor store gone? Mr. Weber was out of a job. Again.

"Where's Richie now?" Pete asked.

"He grabbed a bite here before he swapped places with me in the rowboat."

"Tell him to come by when he gets a chance," Pete said.

He inched forward in the slow-moving line of people

pressed together like pages in a book. Pete ignored the body odors that assaulted his nose. He had never experienced being in need of a handout, never even thought about what other people went through.

When Pete reached the cafeteria, steamy aromas from huge kettles of soup mixed with the people smells. Bottles of milk filled a counter, and loaves of Wonder Bread were piled like cordwood. Pete's stomach rumbled. The few peaches at breakfast had only teased his hunger.

Timmy peered up from his place in front of Pete. "Look!" He pointed. "It's the Army!"

A man in uniform leaned across the counter, so he could see the small boy. "We're National Guard," he said as he placed two bowls of soup on the tray Pete carried. "Our mission is to help."

Carrying trays of food, the Brinkmeyers squeezed through the jam of people, trying not to get jostled. Every drop of soup that sloshed over the bowl's rim meant less to eat.

Mom scouted out a table where they could all sit, while Pete watched to make sure Timmy and Etta didn't get trampled in the crowd. Sister Ignatius would never stand for this kind of noise in their school cafeteria.

Amid the din of voices, scrape of chairs, and tromp of feet, Pete dipped a corner of bread into his tomato soup and took a bite. The soup wasn't as tasty as Mom's homemade, and the thin-sliced bread wasn't as filling as hers, but Pete finished every drop and crumb. And he gulped down his glass of lukewarm milk. He knew he was lucky to get this food.

~~~

After lunch, after fighting the backwash to row across Railroad Street, Pete lifted Timmy from the boat. "You and the kids go back to Aunt Mary's," he told Mom. "I'll be along shortly. I need to do something first."

"We should stay together," Mom said.

"I'll be back soon," Pete promised. "You take the little ones to Aunt Mary's, and I'll be there in time for supper."

"Don't let me down, Pete," she said. The same words Dad had used.

Pete watched Mom and the kids walk in the direction of Aunt Mary's. Mom looked over her shoulder at him twice, and those words seemed etched on her face. *Don't let me down.*

He had tried to do what needed to be done at home, and he'd gotten Mom and the kids to safety. But he couldn't let Richie and his dad do all the tough work. He hadn't forgotten about Dad and Gus. Somebody had to know where they were.

As he headed back to where he'd left the rowboat, he reached into the pocket of the knickers and felt for the bottle cap. *Come on, luck!* he said to himself as he rubbed his thumb across the 7.

CHAPTER 31

THE
COURTHOUSE

To be sure he had the right rowboat, Pete felt for the leak he had patched a week ago. His fingers found it, and it still held. He climbed in and slid the oars into the oarlocks.

Pete was convinced the radio was the best way to find Dad and Gus. Radio station WCMI was underwater, but where were they broadcasting from? He had to find out. Maybe some telephones in town still worked. Gripping the oars, Pete rowed through the massive reach of the flood. Fighting the current. Block after block. Under dark traffic lights. He kept going.

His hands and arms ached and his nose ran. The air felt like water dripping from icicles. Pete blew warm breath into his gloves and held them up to his nose. He had to find WCMI or a working telephone. If Richie and his dad did this every day, Pete could do it as long as it took.

He asked at private homes. No working telephones. He asked at the funeral parlor. No luck.

He asked at the Ford dealership. "We're closed," a man told him. "I'm just the watchman."

"I'm looking for a working telephone," Pete said.

"None here. Maybe at the courthouse."

The powerful current fought him as Pete headed the boat toward Fourth Street. Or where he thought Fourth Street was. He wasn't sure anymore. His mind felt as murky as the floodwater.

He looked for familiar sights, but nothing looked right. Snow still clung to rooftops that barely cleared the water. Which rooftop was which?

He approached taller buildings that marked the business district. But no business could be conducted in all this water.

He began to get his bearings. There! The courthouse dome towered against the sky. He rowed closer to the massive stone building, where the river lapped at first-floor window-sills.

Iron steps to a side door rose out of the water, and Pete tied the boat to the stair rail. Swinging his weary arms to force feeling back into them, he climbed up to the door. He turned the knob. Unlocked.

Pete went inside and walked down a corridor toward the main entrance. On both sides, rooms bustled with people. Like Kingsbury School, the courthouse was being used as a shelter.

In a room off the main hall, a man sat at a desk. Pete

recognized Mr. Allen, a friend of Dad's. And Mr. Allen was talking on a telephone!

Mr. Allen waved him inside. Pete sat on the edge of a chair and bounced his heels up and down.

When Mr. Allen hung up the receiver, he said, "What brings you out in this flood, young Brinkmeyer?"

"Have you seen my dad, Mr. Allen?"

The man shook his head. "Not since the Thanksgiving football game."

"I need to use your telephone. To get in touch with someone at WCMI about broadcasting a message."

"You just found the only working telephone in all of Ironton," Mr. Allen said. "I wish I could help. I've been in touch with WLW in Cincinnati, but I can only call out of town."

"What can I do?" Pete said. "My dad and brother are missing and I need to put out a call to them on the radio."

The man shrugged. "I can tell the folks at WLW, but I don't know how high a priority it'll be for them. Cincinnati is as flooded as we are. I can't call anyone local. Like I said—" The man gestured toward the instrument he had just used. "The only working telephone in all of Ironton."

"I guess we'll have to try WLW," Pete said.

"It's the best we can do," Mr. Allen agreed.

But would it be enough?

CHAPTER 32

RADIO ANNOUNCEMENT

B ack in the rowboat, heading away from the waterlogged business district, Pete thought about going home for some of his own clothes. But he knew the power of the swirling water. Besides, he wasn't sure where home was exactly.

The steeple of Saint Joseph Church rose above rooftops. Using it as a guidepost, he headed away from the riverfront toward Aunt Mary's.

~~~

Aunt Mary's house smelled like meatloaf and wet dog, and Mom's face showed her relief at seeing Pete. But she chewed her lip near bloody, and Pete knew Dad and Gus were on her mind.

"They'll be fine," Aunt Maggie tried to assure her. Mom didn't look convinced.

After a supper of meatloaf that was more bread crumbs than meat, the full household gathered around Aunt Mary's radio to hear the latest news, but news wasn't the only thing Pete hoped to hear.

"Can we listen to WLW?" he asked.

Uncle Mac adjusted the dial, amidst crackles and squawks, until he found WLW.

"At long last," the radio voice declared, "the Ohio River crested today."

Everyone in Aunt Mary's living room cheered.

"Just shy of eighty feet in Cincinnati," the radio continued. "Twenty-eight feet above flood stage and higher than any flood ever recorded in the Ohio River Valley."

The cheers stopped as everyone paused and looked at one another somberly.

"A flood for the ages," said Uncle Mac.

"Damage is extensive," the announcer went on. "Losses will be in the millions of dollars."

Mr. Spurlock whistled through his teeth.

The radio voice continued, "All residents are advised to receive typhoid vaccinations to prevent an outbreak."

The announcer told of fires in Cincinnati due to ruptured fuel tanks. He told about flood damage to Coney Island Amusement Park in Cincinnati, and Crosley Field, where the Cincinnati Redlegs played. He finally moved on to other areas. Louisville, Kentucky. Portsmouth, Ohio.

"What about Ironton?" Pete nearly shouted at the radio.

"There are citizens unaccounted for in many areas," the announcer said. "If anyone has sighted Al or Gus Brinkmeyer from Ironton, Ohio, please report their whereabouts to the Brinkmeyer family, currently residing at the home of Mary Hagen in Ironton."

Pete didn't realize he'd been holding his breath until he breathed out a long "Thank God."

"Amen," chimed in Aunt Mary.

"What do we do now?" Mom asked.

"We wait," Uncle Mac answered.

"And we find out where to get typhoid shots," Aunt Mary added.

~~~

Imogene flicked her tail across Pete's face as he tried to sleep on the floor under Aunt Mary's dining room table. Scruffy peeked around the table leg and made Imogene hiss.

"Shoo!" Pete said, and Scruffy trotted away, but Imogene curled up against Pete's chest, brushing his chin and nose with her tail.

"Dumb cat," he muttered. "Go sleep somewhere else. This is my spot." He nudged the cat with both hands. "Go on. Git!"

But Imogene was undeterred. She curled up against his chest again, and he drew his arms over his face to defend it from her constantly twitching tail.

Pete heard the quiet patter of footsteps on the kitchen linoleum. Aunt Mary was up. It must be nearly dawn.

He crawled out from under the table just as Imogene bolted toward the front door. The door opened softly, and

Imogene found someone else to give her attentions to, rubbing against the trouser legs of the man who entered.

The man bent over, and the arms of his tweed jacket scooped up the cat. "Well, Imogene, how did you end up here?" the voice whispered. Dad's voice!

CHAPTER 33

WHERE'S GUS?

"Dad!" Pete ran to his father, pausing long enough to yell "Dad's here!" up the stairs. "We were so worried about you and Gus." Pete looked onto the porch. "Where *is* Gus?"

Squeals from Etta and the clatter of footsteps on the stairs drowned out any response. Mom leapt from the couch, planting Timmy on his feet. Throwing her arms around her husband, she kissed him soundly, right in front of everybody.

"Al, you're safe. You're here. You're . . ." Mom looked out the door and around the room. "Alone. Where's Gus? Al, where's Gus?"

"I thought he was at home until I heard his name on the radio." Dad's voice quivered. "I hoped they had it wrong."

"I haven't seen him since he left with you," Mom said. "Two Sundays ago."

"I sent him home to tell you I was going to help with evacuees at the post office. How long have you been here?"

"Day before yesterday," Pete said. "Tuesday. When did you send Gus home?"

"Wednesday," Dad answered, "*last* Wednesday. Hank Feldman offered to drop him off for me since he was heading that way." Dad shook his head. "I don't understand. He should have been home more than a week ago."

More than a week ago. Gus had been missing for more than a week, and no one had known. Mom dropped onto the couch, and Aunt Maggie sat beside her, consoling her like folks did at a funeral. But this wasn't a funeral. And Gus couldn't be dead. He couldn't!

Pete knew he wasn't as smart as Gus, but he felt sure there was a sensible answer to his brother's disappearance. He had to make himself think like Gus.

As the other adults gathered around Mom and Dad, Pete's mind delved back to the week before. Gus should have been home on Wednesday. Days blurred into one another, but wasn't Wednesday the night he'd heard that door-slamming sound? Because of the rain, he hadn't gone out to check the garage door. Could it have been Gus?

Dang, Pete, he scolded himself. *You should have checked.*

Pete thought of the spare flashlight that should have been in the Buick. And of his missing bicycle. Maybe Gus *had* come home and taken his Schwinn. Why would Gus do that? Why wouldn't Gus have come inside to give them Dad's message? Was Gus still so mad at Pete, he wouldn't come in the house?

124

But maybe he had. Pete remembered Mom standing in front of the refrigerator and fussing about having less leftover meatloaf than she'd thought. Gus loved meatloaf. And what about those missing oatmeal cookies? Gus's favorite.

That had to be it. Gus had come home. But he hadn't stayed. Why had he left without a word or even a note?

Mom stood up and brushed away tears. "Do I smell toast?" Just like Mom, trying to solve problems with food. But Pete watched her face and knew that food wasn't going to do the job.

Mom helped Aunt Mary to parcel out buttered toast. Pete bit into his toast, while he tried to get his mind to focus.

"Bless us, O Lord . . . ," Aunt Mary began.

Dang! Pete's mind had been elsewhere. The toast clung to the roof of his mouth as he said grace with the others. But grace brought back other memories. Like New Year's dinner. And Venus Marlowe. And those words Pete had tried to erase from his mind. That icky poem in Gus's handwriting.

Gus had gone to see Venus. Pete was sure of it.

"What day did they evacuate Russell, Kentucky?" he asked.

The look on Mom's face seemed to follow Pete's thoughts. "That was mid-week, Wednesday or Thursday," she remembered.

"Russell is like an island now," Uncle Mac said. "Water so high, nobody can get in or out."

125

"He wouldn't have gone there," Mom said. "He wasn't seeing that girl anymore." She squinted at Pete. "Was he?"

"Not that I know of," Pete answered honestly. *But he was definitely thinking about her. And writing her love poems.* Pete's lips nearly spilled out the words he'd seen on that sheet of paper, but he stopped himself.

He had betrayed Gus once before—though not on purpose. He wasn't going to betray him again. He would keep Gus's secret.

PART TWO

GUS

CHAPTER 34

BEWARE
THE
BRINKMEYERS

*D*ad chose me! Gus still couldn't believe it. For as long as he could remember, Dad had selected Pete for work projects. Even though Gus was older and got better grades.

Gus didn't crave doing the greasy, dirty work Dad and Pete liked to do, but he envied that they did it together.

Now, Gus opened the door of Dad's Buick to go with him to fill and pile sandbags with the men from Saint Joe's. Father and son. Together.

Mrs. Taylor's cat, Imogene, rubbed her wet fur against Gus's trouser leg, and he picked her up. "What's the matter, girl?" he said in a tone echoed a second later in her purr.

"Gus!" Dad yelled. "Give me a hand with these shovels."

Gus set Imogene outside the garage.

"I'll spread out a towel in the back seat," Dad said, "and you load these shovels."

The two long-handled shovels clanged together as Gus tried to maneuver them behind the Buick's front seat without brushing them against the upholstery.

"Mind the flashlight," Dad warned. "And our sack lunch."

Gus lifted the flashlight from the Buick's floor and plunked it on the back seat beside the large paper sack that smelled of ham.

Dad climbed into the driver's seat, and Gus trotted around to the passenger side.

"The doors," Dad said, his voice impatient. "You'll need to close the garage doors."

Oh, right, Gus thought. Why hadn't he realized that? Pete was used to doing things with Dad and probably did them without being told.

Dad shifted into reverse and backed out from the garage. As Gus closed the double doors, he looked up at the window of the room he shared with Pete. The light was on. Was Pete still stewing because Dad hadn't picked him?

Dad backed the Buick down the driveway and onto Fifth Street. "This is going to be hard work, Gus," he said. "People's property is at stake. Just think of it as if it were your own things you'd want to protect."

Gus thought of things he'd want protected. His book of Shakespeare's plays that Sister Ignatius had given him for having the top grade in her class. The framed certificate for winning the all-school spelling bee in fifth grade. And the note Venus Marlowe had sent him, thanking him for inviting her to New Year's dinner. *The dinner to end all dinners,* Gus thought.

How could she thank him when his family had treated her the way they had? But that's how Venus was. Thoughtful. Caring. The nicest girl Gus had ever met. And the prettiest, too.

Maybe he shouldn't have invited a nice girl like Venus to a family dinner. He remembered the quote from *Julius Caesar*, "Beware the Ides of March." He wished a soothsayer had warned him, "Beware the Brinkmeyers on January 1."

Gus hadn't heard from Venus since that thank-you note. He had started to telephone her one afternoon, but before he'd dialed the number, Etta had clomped down the stairs and plopped on the sofa to page through *Peter Rabbit*.

He had hurriedly hung up the telephone. Etta never missed a thing. If she found out he was calling Venus, Mom would hear about it soon enough.

He'd tried writing a poem to Venus, but Pete had come into their bedroom, and he'd moved to the dining room table. Timmy had pestered him there. When you lived in a house with five other people, a chance to do *anything* in private rarely happened. *Beware the Brinkmeyers every day.*

CHAPTER 35

THAT OCTOBER DAY

The Buick splashed through puddles as rain streaked across the windshield. When they crossed Main, Gus's eyes locked on the Ironton-Russell Bridge. It was barely visible through the pouring rain, but Gus knew it stretched over the river into Russell, Kentucky, where Venus lived.

Venus. The October day Gus had first met her settled into his mind. He rarely went to football games at Ironton High, the public high school. But Pete was going and asked Gus to join him. Pete always included Gus in whatever he and his friends did. Gus had to give him credit for that.

Gus had felt a sense of history in the stadium, the town's history—and his own. Now the home of Ironton High School's team, the stadium was built for the Ironton Tanks, "an honest-to-goodness, professional football team," according to Dad.

Dad had taken Gus and Pete to watch the Tanks play as soon as his sons were old enough to walk. He'd explained how to keep score and the difference between linebackers and running backs. Pete had absorbed it all—and Gus had pretended to.

If Gus were honest with himself, he hadn't liked football much. He'd even toted a book along to the last Tanks game Dad had taken them to in 1930. That was the year the Tanks folded. Gus didn't miss those football games, but he definitely missed doing things with Dad and Pete.

Gus had a book with him on that October day, too. But he hadn't looked at the book—or the football game. He'd watched the beautiful blonde girl, trying to work up the gumption to speak to her.

At halftime, he'd forced himself to say hello.

"I noticed you weren't watching the game either," she'd said with a smile. "Football isn't my top choice for an October day, but my friends convinced me it's the place to meet good-looking boys."

Did Venus think he was good-looking?

It didn't matter. They'd started talking and couldn't stop. They'd talked about books and history and whether popcorn tasted better with or without butter. Gus had never met a girl who cared what he had to say. And he liked learning about Venus, watching the way her mouth formed words, hearing the soft lilt of her voice.

"I wish this fool rain would stop." Dad's deep tone yanked Gus back to the present. "It makes driving treacherous." Dad's hands tapped nervously on the steering wheel.

Parking the Buick at the curb near the liquor store, Dad

grabbed the shovels from the back seat. Joey Feldman and Ralph Mackie from Gus's class huddled with a group of men, sheltering from the rain beneath the awning of the Moore building. Beside them, a pile of sand stood higher than the awning.

"It's the Brinkmeyers!" Joey's dad called out. "More workers. Glad you could join us, Al, and glad you brought Pete."

"I'm not Pete. I'm Gus."

Sure, Dad had brought Pete on other work projects, and these men knew Pete. But it wasn't as if Gus had never shown his face before. Sometimes Gus felt invisible. But Venus never made him feel that way.

CHAPTER 36

SAND AND TRUCKS

A pile of empty sandbags sat on the tailgate of a Ford truck, and Dad handed Gus a shovel. All the men fell into place, seeming to know exactly what to do. Gus watched for a second, before acting as though he'd filled sandbags all his life.

Joey Feldman held open an empty bag, while Gus shoveled sand into it. When it was filled, Joey tied it closed and threw it up to a man who stood in the bed of another truck.

Bag after bag. Shovelful after shovelful. By the time the pile of sand was reduced to gritty remnants on the sidewalk, Gus's hands wore blisters, and one of them was bleeding.

Gus sucked blood from his finger as he leaned on the handle of his shovel. It was past noon, but nobody mentioned lunch. Some of the men clustered under the awning of the Moore building and lit cigarettes.

One man passed around cups and a large Thermos jug filled with coffee. Gus didn't really like coffee, but holding the steaming cup warmed his hands—and stung the open blister.

The rain hadn't let up all morning, and Gus was soaked clean to his innards. Cold water had drizzled every place water could drizzle. Down his back, inside his boots, and right through his hat. Maybe being chosen over Pete wasn't such an honor after all. What Gus wanted now was to be home and dry.

Dad motioned him over to the Buick, and Gus climbed in. He reached for the towel that had protected the back seat from the shovels. He rubbed his hair as dry as he could get it and dried the back of his neck as far as he could reach.

Dad handed him a sandwich from the sack Mom had packed. One sandwich barely eased the emptiness in his stomach.

"Are there more?" Gus asked.

"We'll save those for later," Dad said.

Gus's stomach rumbled in protest. He had worked like a chain-gang prisoner all morning. The only thing missing was the shackles. Did Pete truly *like* this kind of work?

~~~

After lunch, the men followed the five trucks they'd filled with sandbags. The trucks stopped at the low end of Second Street, not far from the riverbank, where water surged past, the mighty Ohio running at full speed.

The rain lashed the river, whipping it into an angry monster that threatened to consume Ironton's West End.

This wasn't about being with Dad now. It was about defending people and property from the river's clutches.

Men climbed to the beds of the trucks and tossed sandbags to those on the ground, like a strange game of catch. A man tossed a sandbag to another man, who tossed it to another, who lined the bags along the curb. When the line reached the end of the block, the tossing continued, and another row of bags was heaped on top of the first.

Blood seeped through Gus's glove where another blister had broken open, but he had no time to stop. As soon as he draped a sandbag on the pile, another was tossed to him.

When every sandbag was unloaded and stacked, the men followed the trucks back to where they'd started. Gus was tired and his feet felt like blocks of ice, but he had done the job. In spite of pain, rain, and cold, he had battled the mighty river.

He wanted to climb into the Buick and eat another sandwich, or better yet, go home for Mom's hot vegetable soup or meatloaf. He couldn't wait to hear Dad tell Mom he was proud of Gus. Gus was proud of himself. He was sure Pete couldn't have done better.

Before he had time to walk to the Buick, a noise broke through the constant sound of rain on the brick street. Gus looked up through raindrops still clinging to his eyelashes. A dump truck chugged down the street with another load of sand.

CHAPTER 37

SERPENT'S TOOTH

The line of sandbags was three bags thick, as high as Gus's chest, and longer than a football field before the men stopped for the night. Gus figured it was well past midnight as he followed Dad to a room at the American Legion hall, his feet so wet and cold he couldn't feel them.

Dad carried the sack of sandwiches from the Buick. Lunch had been twelve hours ago, and Gus was ravenous. He wolfed down a sandwich without even tasting the ham and cheese. Before he could ask for another, Dad extended half of his own sandwich to a man at the next table.

"Hey, Al," Mr. Feldman called. "These are for you and your boy." He tossed a couple blankets in their direction.

He can't remember my name, Gus thought. Almost as bad as being invisible.

Dad spread his blanket on the floor near the radiator. "We'll bed down here where it's warmer. All we have is the floor. Seems they moved their cots to a school, so they can use it as a shelter."

"The floor's fine," Gus said, unfolding his blanket.

He noticed a line of men, waiting to use the coin-operated telephone. "Will you call Mom and tell her we're staying over?"

"At this hour?" Dad said. "And let the telephone's jangle wake the kids? Your mother wouldn't want me wasting a hard-earned nickel just to tell her I don't know how long this will take."

"But don't you want to check on things at home?"

"I don't have to worry about home," Dad said. "Pete's there. He can handle things as well as I can."

Gus had been easing down to the floor as Dad spoke, but he landed hard when the impact of Dad's words hit him. Dad hadn't left Pete at home because Gus would be a good worker, or because Dad wanted to do something with Gus. Dad needed Pete at home because Pete was the reliable one. The one who *can handle things as well as I can.*

Gus stretched out on the wood floor. He was more tired than he'd ever been, but he wasn't going to let Dad know. He wouldn't let Dad think he was less than Pete.

But Dad's words were harder than the floor. *Pete's there. He can handle things as well as I can.* They ran through Gus's head and kept him awake.

Julius Caesar couldn't have felt worse when Brutus stabbed him, Gus thought.

~~~

Dad nudged Gus awake before dawn. "Back to work," Dad said.

139

Gus felt as if his eyes had barely closed, and his socks were still damp—and stiff. He groped in his pockets for the clean pair he'd brought. They were wet, too.

"Why'd you leave your clean socks in your pockets while we worked in the rain?" Dad said, as he pulled on his own dry socks. "You should've left them in the car."

It hadn't even crossed Gus's mind to take the socks out of his pockets. He hadn't anticipated how wet he'd get. Besides, tugging on wet shoes and boots wouldn't let the socks stay dry for long.

Gus winced as he pushed himself from the floor. Resting his arm muscles overnight had only heightened the ache in them. But Dad's look of disapproval over the socks was a greater pain.

"I brought breakfast," Mr. Mackie called, toting in a large box of rolls. "Donated day-olds from the bakery."

Yesterday, Gus had shoveled sand and hefted sandbags. Today, his muscles throbbed just lifting a roll to his mouth. The rolls were hard to bite into, but they helped to ease the empty place in Gus's belly.

But nothing ebbed that other emptiness. Gus tried to put Dad's words out of his mind, but they played in his mind like a stuck phonograph record. *Pete can handle things. Pete can handle things.*

Gus seethed. All his good grades. All his hard work yesterday. Absolutely unappreciated.

140

Shakespeare's *King Lear* dropped into his head. "How sharper than a serpent's tooth it is to have a thankless child." But what about a thankless parent?

CHAPTER 38

NATIONAL GUARD

G us draped his dirty socks on the radiator in the Legion hall, before going out to fill and stack sandbags in pouring rain. Though *surely* they would go home before the day was over.

He worked side by side with Joey Feldman. Joey was in his class at school, but Gus hardly knew him. Gus usually kept to himself. Not that he didn't want to be friends. He just wanted other people to make the first move. And they hadn't. Gus's friends were Pete's friends, friends like Richie Weber, because Pete always included Gus.

Gus had to admit it. Pete was a good brother. Or he used to be. The beef with Pete had begun at New Year's dinner. Pete should have kept his trap shut, instead of probing into Venus's business. Pete claimed he'd been asking polite questions. And maybe he was, but the answers had forced Venus from Gus's life. He hadn't seen her in more than two weeks. *Dang that Pete!*

At the thought, Gus tossed a sandbag a bit too hard and nearly knocked Joey off his feet.

"Sorry," Gus said, but the word was lost in the driving rain and splash of water against the sandbags. The pouring rain and overflowing river seemed to be in cahoots. The river taunted with its advance, while rain laughed at their efforts. There would be no going home today. The sandbag wall had to be higher.

Gus ignored bleeding blisters on his hands and new blisters being rubbed on his soaked feet. He had to keep on. This wall was the only defense for folks on Second Street. It needed to protect their possessions. Objects as valuable as Shakespeare's plays, framed certificates, and thank-you notes from pretty girls.

But the river surged closer, its current churning, its muddy water stealing toward Second Street, the street where Richie lived.

~~~

Gus and the others kept up the struggle to stay ahead of the rising water. They worked from before dawn until midnight, when they dragged themselves up to the Legion hall to drop exhausted onto the floor, to catch a few hours of sleep before resuming the battle. Every night, Gus left his wet socks on the radiator, so each day offered dry ones. Dirty and stiff, but dry.

By the third day, everyone smelled like dirty socks, and men's whiskers spoke of passing time. Even Joey Feldman sported the birth of a mustache and a bit of peach fuzz on his chin. Gus rubbed his own chin. Smooth as an apple's peel. Likely Pete would have a full beard before Gus grew his first whisker.

Rain continued to fall, and the mighty Ohio slapped at the sandbags. Each day was more discouraging than the one before, as the river rose higher on the wall. It was inevitable. Sooner or later, the river would have its way.

By late Wednesday afternoon, the river threatened to breach the sandbags. In the restroom, Gus stuffed toilet paper in his sock to keep his shoe from breaking open the blister on his heel. He thrust his feet into wet shoes and boots, and went back outside just as the National Guard showed up.

"We're clearing the area," a Guardsman told them. He raised his voice and told everyone, "Grab your gear and move your vehicles. This building is being evacuated."

"But the sandbags?" Gus said.

"They won't stop the river much longer," the man said.

After all Gus and the men had endured, the wall would be abandoned to surrender to the river. Gus felt defeated.

"We've been evacuating people up and down both sides of the river," the man said. "We evacuated parts of Portsmouth, Ashland, and Russell."

Russell? Had Venus been evacuated? "Shelters where?" he asked.

"We're setting up shelters in schools and the post office."

"The post office?" Dad repeated.

Most of the men were happy to be able to go home and check on their families. "We gave it our best shot," Mr. Feldman said.

But Gus couldn't think about home. "Where are the Russell evacuees?"

The man's look was dismissive. "In shelters in Russell."

"I know my way around the post office as well as anyone," Dad interrupted. "I'll see if I can help settle evacuees there."

"You want me to go, too?" Gus asked.

"Hank!" Dad called to Mr. Feldman. "You and Joey heading home? Can you drop off my boy Gus?"

"Tell him to get a wiggle on," Mr. Feldman said.

"Hurry and fetch your stuff and go with Hank," Dad said. "When you get home, tell your mother what's going on."

Gus didn't have much to fetch from upstairs—one pair of damp, dirty socks. And from the Buick, just his spare underwear. The radiator had served well for his socks, but underwear was different. He'd kept them in the Buick after that first day of pulling on damp shorts.

He groped along the front seat, but couldn't find them. He checked the back seat. He looked under the towel. Not there either. But Dad's flashlight was. He shined it under the seat. Nothing. He beamed the flashlight between the seat cushion and the padded seatback. Something was there. He squeezed in his hand and pulled out his shorts. How had his underwear gotten wedged way down there? He slipped them into his pocket just as Dad called to him from the sidewalk.

Dad frowned. "Hank's ready to leave," he said. "You can't keep him waiting when he's doing us a favor."

Dad's impatient face made Gus long for the days of feeling invisible.

"Don't forget to tell your mother where I am," Dad said.

Gus nodded and realized he still held Dad's flashlight. He wasn't going to take it back to the Buick now. He had seen enough of Dad's disappointed face.

CHAPTER 39

ALMOST HOME

Mr. Feldman's windshield wipers didn't work well, and he leaned forward and squinted to see through the rain.

Gus sat in the back seat and wondered where Venus might evacuate to, if she did. A Kentucky post office? A Kentucky school? Maybe she was still at home. He had to find out.

The Feldman car crawled up Center Street and approached Fifth. "You can let me out here, Mr. Feldman, and I'll walk the rest of the way," Gus said. "You and Joey need to get home."

Mr. Feldman seemed reluctant, but grateful at the same time. He slowed the car as though he were considering. "I *would* like to get home in time to hear what the evening news says about the President's inauguration, but I ought to take you right to your door."

"I'll be fine," Gus assured him. "Thanks for the ride."

He opened the car door before the man had time to change his mind.

The wind wrestled the car door from his grip, but Gus managed to get out and close it. Rain pelted him, as Gus loped down Fifth Street into wind that wanted to push him back. His muscles ached and his eyes were tired. He tucked his chin to keep rain from pummeling his face.

Only a few blocks and he'd be home. Gus was finished with sandbags and sleeping on the floor. At home, he could put on dry clothes for the first time in four days. He could eat until he was full as a 4-H pig, curl up in his warm bed, and sleep for two days straight. But he had to call Venus first. He had to know for sure she was safe.

The sky blackened from rainy-day gray to nighttime dark as home loomed in front of Gus. Lights were on in the living room, and he headed up the drive and around back to the sunroom.

His foot was on the bottom step, and he heard the family's voices inside. His hand reached for the knob.

He'd never get a chance to call Venus with all the family around. Mom didn't approve of her, and the little kids would tattle. And Pete? Yes, Pete was a good brother, but could Gus trust him with his most important secret?

He pulled back his hand from the knob. He had to call her from somewhere else, away from prying eyes. Where could he go? There was a pay telephone at Wally's Corner Store, but Wally's would be closed by now. Wally and his wife lived above the store. Maybe they'd let him in to use the telephone.

He turned back into the wind and rain and headed toward Fourth Street. The distance to Wally's had never seemed so far as he leaned into the tempest howling around him. Each step seemed to get him nowhere as the wind slowed his progress.

~~~

Wally's store was dark as Gus had expected, but no light shined from the windows on the second floor either. No one was home or they were already in bed.

Gus leaned his forehead against the store's windowpane. Cupping his hands around his face to shut out the porch light across the street, he could see the pay telephone on the wall.

He considered for a moment pounding on Wally's door in case they were inside. But if he woke them from a sound sleep, they would tell Mom and Dad. How would he explain his need for a telephone?

What other telephone could he use? One where no one would overhear his call? Or tell his parents? Saint Joe's Church! If Father Gloekner overheard him talking to Venus, he wouldn't be allowed to tell, would he? Didn't priests take vows about keeping secrets?

CHAPTER 40

CALLING VENUS

Walking to Saint Joe's was an undertaking in *nice* weather. Fifteen blocks from home. Eleven blocks from Wally's. In this storm, it would be overwhelming. But Gus couldn't go home without checking on Venus. He needed to know she was all right.

Again, he bent into the wind and rain. He plodded along the puddled sidewalks. With every step, he pictured Venus's face.

He distracted himself from the chill seeping through his wet trousers and coat by thinking up poems. Poems about wind and rain. Poems about dark, starless skies. *Life without Venus is like a sky without stars.*

When he finally reached the church, he was drenched. His hands and feet were freezing. His knuckles stung right through his gloves when he rapped on the rectory door.

Father Gloekner opened the door, an overhead light glinting off his bald head. Gus almost didn't recognize the parish priest, who stood in the doorway in a bathrobe. A bathrobe, for crying out loud! Pajama legs showed beneath its hem. Gus had never imagined the priest in something other than his black cassock or Sunday vestments. And always, always that stiff white collar.

Gus couldn't seem to speak as the old priest ushered him inside. "Come in where it's dry, Augustine," Father Gloekner said in his paternal tone. "Is someone ill? Has someone died?"

The parish priest got his name right. Of course. This was one time being confused for Pete could have made things easier if this visit was ever mentioned to his parents.

Gus shook his head and found his voice, which came out in a squeak. "Nothing like that. I just need to use your telephone. May I?" he added in a more normal pitch.

Gus's clothes dripped a trail of small puddles on the rectory floor as he followed Father Gloekner to a room where the priest's hand motioned to a telephone on a desk.

"Could I use it in private?" Gus screaked out.

"I will leave you to make your call," the priest said, "but you know you are never alone. There are no secrets from God."

But God won't tell Mom and Dad, Gus thought as he dialed Venus's number. Rotary dial telephones had been introduced in Ironton less than a year ago. Gus was relieved not to have to talk to a switchboard operator. The fewer people who knew about this call, the better.

The telephone rang and rang. Did that mean Venus and her mother had evacuated? What else could it mean? They had to be safe. Gus was about to hang up when Venus's voice said, "Hello."

She was home. It was good to hear her voice for the first time since New Year's Day. He found himself tongue-tied.

"Hello," Venus said again.

Gus had to speak. "I thought maybe you went to a shelter," he said. *What a stupid thing to say,* he berated himself.

"Gus!" Venus sounded happy. "I haven't heard from you. Did you get my note?"

"I did," he said. If only she knew how much that note meant to him. How much *she* meant to him. But he couldn't tell her, and he couldn't say he'd been forbidden to see her. "I was worried about you," he said. "I heard Russell is flooded and folks are being evacuated."

"We're off school until the flood goes down," she said, "but our house is safe. We're far enough from the river that . . ."

A voice sounded in the background, and Venus shushed the person who spoke.

"I miss you," Gus said and waited for her to say she missed him, too. But she didn't. Whatever she said was muffled, like her hand was over the telephone.

"Are you going to evacuate?" Gus asked.

"No," she said. "We'll stay here."

"I could come over," he offered. Even though he knew Mom would never allow it.

"No," she insisted. "We're all fine. Don't come over."

Gus heard the background voice again. A male voice.

"Hush," Venus said to the voice.

Who was that? Venus and her mom lived alone, didn't they?

"I have to hang up now, Gus," Venus said.

The telephone clicked, and she was gone.

Gus stared at the silent receiver. Who did the male voice belong to? Why did she hang up so quickly? And why did she say, "We're *all* fine?" *All*, not *both*. Who else was there?

CHAPTER 41

SNEAKING

G us thanked Father Gloekner for the use of his telephone and left before the priest had a chance to ask questions.

The cold wind pierced him again as he stepped outside. He avoided looking toward the river. Though he likely wouldn't see much in the dark, Gus knew it was still rising. If he didn't look, he might convince himself it was just the usual Ironton flood. But water slashing the sandbag wall was permanently burned into his mind. It haunted him. And so did Venus's giving him the bum's rush.

Walking the fifteen blocks back to Fifth Street had the wind at Gus's back, pushing him along.

Before he had much time to stew over Venus, he was home. The house was dark except for Mom's bedroom window. As he walked up the drive and around to the back, he noticed Pete's light was on, too.

Ever so quietly, he opened the sunroom door, and stepped into the dark house. Stealing through the kitchen like a burglar on the prowl, he avoided every squeaky floorboard.

A pan of meatloaf in the refrigerator reminded him how hungry he was. He peeled back its waxed paper and pulled off a thick slice with his hand. Eating it cold, he nearly dropped it when the Kelvinator kicked on and startled him. As it began its familiar hum, he almost expected Mom or Pete to come downstairs and catch him red-handed. Tomato-sauce red. But the noise of the refrigerator was no cause for alarm. He had to remain calm.

He dipped into the hand-painted cookie tin. Oatmeal cookies! His favorite! His warm bed was just upstairs. But Pete was awake and so was Mom. He wasn't ready to let them know he was home. The call with Venus had him on edge.

He wriggled out of his wet coat and stretched out on the picnic-table bench, laying his head on his bunched-up coat. The hard bench was no worse than the Legion hall floor.

Something jolted him awake hours later. He saw Dad's flashlight lying on its side on the table. He must have knocked it over in his sleep. He listened for footsteps from upstairs, but heard only the howling of the wind and his own breathing.

He padded into the kitchen to check the clock. After midnight. He couldn't show up at Venus's this late, but he knew he had to go. First thing in the morning, he'd head to Russell. He'd call Mom from there to tell her where Dad went. He wouldn't tell her where he was calling from.

But he couldn't let himself fall asleep on the bench again

and risk being discovered. He had to hide somewhere for the next few hours.

He slid on his wet coat and filled his pockets with oatmeal cookies. Carrying Dad's flashlight, he opened the door to outside. Before he could ease it closed, the wind snatched it from his grasp. He reached for it, but the wind was quicker, and slammed the door with a loud *Bang!*

He hurried to the garage, stopping just outside its side door, where he could look up to the house's second floor. Pete's light went on. He slipped inside the garage and held his breath. He didn't turn on the garage light, just stood in the dark, hiding like a prowler. The only sounds were wind and rain.

He finally opened the door, holding tight to the knob, and peeked out. Pete's light was off.

Gus closed the door. Halfway across the garage's concrete floor, he bumped into something in the dark. *Ow!* Flicking on the flashlight, he saw Dad's rowboat in the middle of the garage!

"What the—" Gus remembered when Dad used to take him and Pete fishing in this boat. They'd row down toward Portsmouth and stop at a place where Dad said the catfish waited for him. "Just begging to be Friday supper," Dad would say.

It had been years since they'd done that. Gus was never much of a fisherman, so he'd take a book along and read

Rime of the Ancient Mariner or *Moby-Dick*. Was that why Dad quit taking Gus? Had he assumed Gus was bored?

That didn't matter now. Dad was at the post office. Pete was in bed. And the boat was here. Smack dab in the middle of the garage. Gus took off most of his wet clothes and draped them—and his spare socks and underwear—across the boat's benches to dry. He curled up on the floor of the boat and pulled his damp coat over him. It wasn't the worst bed he'd had this week.

CHAPTER 42

MORNING IN THE GARAGE

G us slept to the *whoosh* of the wind and unending patter of rain on the garage roof. He woke to the jingly *clink* of bottles, as the milkman left them in the crate on the sunroom steps.

Crawling out from under his coat, Gus noticed the skin of his arms and legs had the imprint of the bottom of the boat splayed across them. He slid into his spare shorts and his just-barely-damp trousers and shirt.

If he went into the house, Mom would make him breakfast and fuss over him to eat more. He could take a hot shower and put on clean clothes, but checking on Venus wouldn't be possible. Making sure Venus was safe was worth the discomfort of damp fabric.

Gus was hungry. The oatmeal cookies he'd slipped into his pocket were damp lumps, but he turned his pocket inside out and dumped every crumb into his mouth. It wasn't as good as a hot meal, but it took the edge off his hunger.

On tiptoe, he peered out the high windows of the main

garage doors, but couldn't see clearly through the rain-streaked glass. He pressed his ear to the door to listen for sounds other than rain. He heard Mom come out to get the milk. He heard Pete leave for school. He heard two honks of a horn and knew Mr. Brunner and his daughter were sitting at the curb, signaling for Etta. Mr. Brunner always dropped the girls at school on his way to work at the newspaper.

Now Mom and Timmy were the only ones home. If Gus timed it just right, he could slip out when Mom would be in the kitchen. The kitchen window looked out on the driveway, and he could dodge around the other side of the house.

Gus shivered, but he didn't want to put on his coat until it had more time to dry.

The sound of scratching and meowing came from outside the garage door. Imogene. Gus opened the door just a smidgen, and the cat scrambled in. She brushed against his trouser leg, but he didn't bend down to pick her up until she wiped most of the moisture off her fur.

He sat on the rowboat seat holding the cat. "What do you think, Imogene? Am I a sap for sleeping in the garage when my bed is so close? Love can make a fella do strange things." Imogene's answer was a scratchy tongue on his cheek.

When he heard Mrs. Taylor on her back porch calling for Imogene, he opened the door and let Imogene outside. He counted out sixty seconds for the neighbor to let the cat into the house before he slipped on his almost-dry coat.

It would be a long walk to Venus's. Maybe he could ride his bicycle. He almost never rode it anymore, but it sure would beat walking in the rain. He reached for the handlebars to pull it away from the wall, but the tire was flat as a pancake. It had been that way for a while, and he'd forgotten to get it fixed.

Pete never forgot about stuff like that. And there sat Pete's bicycle to prove it. But Pete wouldn't ride it in this weather. Gus could take it and have it back long before Pete missed it.

CHAPTER 43

RUSSELL

The Schwinn's balloon tires splayed water behind them as Gus raced down Main Street toward the Ironton-Russell Bridge. The bike slowed as water rose higher on its wheels. The bridge stretched well above the surface of the river, but floodwater was everywhere. It lapped at the ramp to the bridge. In the gray light and steady rain, Gus couldn't tell how deep it was. Would he be able to get back once he crossed it?

"That you, Gus Brinkmeyer?" a voice called.

Gus looked around but didn't see anyone—until he looked *under* the bridge. Beneath the near end of the bridge, Richie Weber sat in a rowboat, both hands on the oars. He rowed out from under the bridge and into the dreary daylight.

"What'cha doing, Richie?"

"Just staying out'a the rain for a minute. I been checking the riverbank to rescue folks or see if anyone needs supplies. It was Pete's idea."

Of course it was.

"You want to join me?" Richie asked.

"Maybe later," Gus said. "You rescued anybody from over in Russell?"

"Nah. I didn't rescue anybody yet. Today's my first day doing this. Only person wanted something fetched for 'em was Old Lady Knapp, who wanted Pepto Bismol from Rist Drugs. You can't take a rowboat across anyhow. Current's too swift. Too dangerous. Only boats crossing it are Coast Guard. I s'pose they're gonna close this bridge before much longer. The ramp'll be submerged."

"So if I cross the bridge, how long you think I have before my way home will be under water?" Gus asked.

"Can't say for sure, but you'd be crazy to try it. Water's getting deeper by the minute."

"Then I'd better not waste another minute."

Gus pumped the bicycle pedals and headed onto the bridge. He didn't look back at Richie or his rowboat, didn't look down at the river he knew was creeping further up its banks. His eyes centered on the bridge in front of him.

Once he was safely across, he wasn't quite sure where Venus's house was. He had been there just twice, when Dad picked her up and dropped her off on that fateful New Year's Day. But her address was etched firmly in his mind, right beside her telephone number and the scent of her blonde curls that bounced every time she looked up at him.

After a few tries, Gus finally found Boyd Street. Venus's

162

street. It was nearly as far from the river on the Kentucky side as Fifth Street was on the Ohio side. He hoped it was as high above flood level. Had he been foolish to worry?

Boyd Street's houses were somewhat weathered, probably at least thirty years old, most painted gray or white. A few were boarded up. Victims of the Depression.

Built on a mound between two-story homes, a single-level brown house gave the appearance of being larger than it was. Its number was carved into a small wood sign hanging from the porch roof. This was it!

Gus dropped Pete's Schwinn on the soggy winter-dead lawn and strode up five wooden steps to a covered stoop. But once he reached the front door, he hesitated. Venus had told him not to come. Yet here he stood, that male voice still gnawing in his brain. He took a deep breath and rapped on the door.

Fingers pried between the slats of Venetian blinds, and someone peered out. Gus heard footsteps from inside and the door opened a few inches. Venus.

"Gus, I told you not to come." Her hand slipped through the opening and pushed him away, lingering for a brief second on the front of his wet coat.

"I had to see you," he said, reaching for her hand.

She hesitated a mere moment before she snatched her hand away. "Please, Gus. Go home." She closed the door firmly between them.

CHAPTER 44

TELEPHONE

Gus didn't move. He couldn't. Telling him not to come over was one thing, but shutting the door in his face was definite. She didn't want him here. Likely didn't want him at all. Maybe she had already replaced him with the boy whose voice he'd heard on the telephone.

What had he been thinking? Believing a pretty girl was interested in a bookworm like him? He thought back, remembered their lengthy conversations, remembered the feel of her fingers entwined with his as they'd laughed to-gether at the *Three Stooges*. She had liked him. *Had!* Up until that New Year's dinner. The day Pete ruined his life.

But was this really Pete's fault? Gus should never have invited Venus for a holiday dinner, for any dinner with his family. He knew how they were, knew Aunt Mary's bias against anyone who wasn't Catholic. He should have warned Pete. Would Pete have kept his secret if he'd asked him to? He hadn't asked. He'd never know. Gus was the one who'd invited her. Like a lamb to the slaughter.

The sound of rain plinking off the roof above the stoop seemed to prod him. Determined, he rapped on the door again.

"Gus," Venus said through that same small gap between door and jamb, "you can't be here." Her eyes glistened. Were those tears? Had he made her cry?

"Venus, I'm sorry. Sorry for everything. Sorry for letting my family offend you at New Year's dinner. It's all my fault. Please, don't stay angry."

The gap opened a bit wider and Venus slipped outside.

"I'm not angry," she said. "And I understand about the dinner. Your parents think I'm wrong for you." She sighed. "Trust me. I understand about parents who try too hard."

"You're not wrong for me, Venus. I don't care what they think. You're the best thing that ever happened to me."

A blush reddened her cheeks. "I like you, too, Gus."

"Will you still go out with me?"

"Yes, but how about we wait until it quits raining?"

Relief washed over him, and he laughed. He took her hand and held it between both of his. He didn't know how he'd be able to keep seeing her, but he had to try. Maybe he could convince Mom and Dad . . .

"Oh, thunder!" Gus smacked his own forehead. "I was supposed to tell my mom where my dad is, and I forgot." He was already going to be in trouble, even without bringing up Venus. "She's going to wonder why he . . . why *we* haven't come home yet. Can I use your telephone?"

"Just a minute," Venus said, slipping through that crack in the door as easily as sliding a letter into a mail slot.

Gus waited on the porch. She still liked him, was willing to keep going out with him.

Venus opened the door again, wider this time, and motioned Gus inside. "You have to hurry," she said. "My mother needs to make an important call."

She led Gus to the telephone, but when he picked up the receiver, nothing happened. Perhaps someone from the party line was already using the telephone?

"Hello?" he said. "Hello? Is someone on the line?" No answer. He pressed the cradle up and down repeatedly. "Hello?"

He turned to Venus. "I think your telephone's dead."

Venus took the receiver. "Hello?" She plunked the receiver in its cradle. "Dead as a door nail."

"Now your mother can't make her call."

"Her what?"

"You said she has an important call to make."

"Oh, I nearly forgot." Venus looked flustered. "I guess she'll have to try later. Don't worry about it. Go home and give your mother the message from your father."

"You're right." Gus remembered Richie's warning. "I have to cross the bridge while I still can." How high had the water risen around the bridge's ramps?

Gus hurried down the five steps and retrieved Pete's bicycle from the lawn. He turned to wave to Venus.

166

"Be careful," she called.

He pedaled back to the bridge, but before he approached the ramp, he saw the wide stream of water between him and the bridge. There was no way to cross it.

CHAPTER 45

TOOLSHED

G us straddled the bicycle and stared at the bridge through the pouring rain. It was so close, but the water between him and the bridge seemed to widen right before his eyes. The river was swollen to twice its usual width. He looked across to the Ironton side. It might as well be a hundred miles away. There was no way to go home. No way to give Dad's message to Mom.

Rain whipped Gus's face, and he turned away from the wind. He was already as wet as a goldfish in a bowl. And as cold as the frozen catfish in the ice chest at Wally's store.

He headed the Schwinn toward Venus's.

But she hadn't wanted him there.

Her voice dropped into his head. *I understand about parents who try too hard.* Maybe Venus's mother didn't like her daughter keeping company with a Catholic any more than Gus's parents wanted him seeing a Protestant. Was that why Venus was reluctant to let him inside? Because of her mother? He couldn't put Venus on the spot.

168

He braked the bike. Where could he escape the downpour? He was already on Boyd Street, but he steered clear of Venus's house.

Through the pelting rain, he gaped at a boarded-up house. Could he break in to get out of the icy wind and rain? All Ten Commandments ran through his mind. *Thou shalt not break into an abandoned house* was not on the list, but he knew it fit into one of the others somewhere.

He stared at the house, his skin numb from the weather, his nose running and freezing above his lip. As he looked around to see if anyone was watching, he caught sight of a doghouse behind the boarded-up house. Was he desperate enough to crawl into a doghouse?

Dropping the Schwinn on the driveway, he cautiously headed to the doghouse. He glanced repeatedly over his shoulder to make sure no one saw him. But the neighborhood seemed deserted. Likely the rain kept everyone indoors.

When he rounded the corner of the house, he spotted a toolshed with its door hanging crooked from one hinge. He wouldn't need to resort to a doghouse after all. He slipped into the shed and pulled the lopsided door behind him.

Old spider webs clung to a broken sawhorse, and rain pounded the roof. A trickle of water spilled through a hole in one corner, but a higher spot in the ground provided a dry space—a space just big enough for Gus. The shed wasn't warm, but he was out of the wind.

Already drenched to the skin, his arms and legs were

gooseflesh. And his teeth chattered. He slid off his soggy coat and used it as a blanket. He wiped his nose on a spare sock from his pocket and slipped off his shoes to keep them from rubbing his blisters. The chill from the dirt floor seeped through the soles of his feet and seat of his trousers and permeated his whole body. He curled into a ball and wrapped his arms around himself to get warm, but still he shivered.

The floor at the Legion hall didn't seem so bad anymore. At least the room had a radiator. The bottom of a rowboat had been uncomfortable, but home had been just across the yard if he became desperate enough. Now the river had him trapped in Russell. In a toolshed!

CHAPTER 46

OUT OF THE RAIN

"Gus?" A loud whisper. "Gus Brinkmeyer? Are you here?"

Gus heard his name, recognized the voice. He'd been asleep and needed a few seconds to remember where he was. Curled up in his coat in a freezing toolshed in Russell, Kentucky.

"Gus?" the voice called again.

He unfolded his stiff arms and legs and pulled on his shoes. Stretching up to his full height, he poked his head from the shed. "Venus? What are you doing here?"

Her blonde hair hung wet and limp, but she had never looked more beautiful. "Oh, Gus, thank God you're all right! I've been looking for you all morning."

"Morning? What day is it?"

"Friday, January 22. Are you sure you're all right?"

Gus swung his arms to work the kinks from them and raised up and down on his toes in an attempt to warm his legs.

"Me and Mom heard on the radio they closed the Ironton-Russell Bridge. I hoped you'd crossed in time, but I was worried." She threw her arms around him. "I was scared something happened to you."

He put his arm around her. "I didn't mean to frighten you."

She leaned into him. "With the telephone out, I couldn't call, so I've been looking for you just in case. Then I saw your bicycle in the driveway here."

"When I couldn't cross the bridge, I didn't go back to your house because I didn't want to upset your mother. I figured she doesn't approve of your going out with a Catholic."

"A Catholic? Is that what you thought?"

"You didn't want me to come inside, and you didn't let me meet her. What was I supposed to think? Saying she had to make a call was just to hurry me off, wasn't it?"

Venus laughed, and Gus held her close.

"When did you eat last?" she asked.

He had to think back. Meatloaf and oatmeal cookies when he'd made it home on Wednesday evening. "Cookie crumbs yesterday morning," he said.

She pulled away from him and took his hand. "Grab your bicycle and we'll go to my house."

Pushing Pete's Schwinn, Gus walked beside Venus in the rain. Nobody else was in sight, not even watching from windows. It was as if they were the only two people on Earth.

"Did the river rise much overnight?" Gus asked through chattering teeth.

Venus nodded slowly. "The radio said Russell's like an island. No one can get in or out."

~~~

Gus took off his boots and left them beside the door. His feet were numb.

Venus led him to an easy chair beside the telephone.

"I'll get your chair wet," Gus protested.

"Don't worry about that." She spread a purple afghan over him, and he tugged its scratchy warmth around him.

"How about a cup of tea or coffee?" she offered.

"Tea would be nice," he said.

While the tea brewed, Venus brought him a slice of chocolate cake. He wolfed it down in three bites, leaning over the plate to avoid dropping crumbs on the purple afghan.

"Iff's good," he said, as best he could with a full mouth.

"Thanks. I'll get you another piece. I baked it for my . . . for my mom. It's her favorite."

Venus went to the kitchen, and Gus slipped off his shoes and sodden socks. Drawing his shriveled-skin feet under the afghan, he tried to rub feeling into them.

The front door flew open, and a woman carrying a cardboard box of groceries stepped inside, kicking the door closed with her knee.

Gus hurriedly plopped his feet on the floor.

"The river's getting really high," the woman said, "but

the American Legion is giving out food. Did you hear me, Venus?" she called out.

The woman walked right past Gus before she finally saw him around the bottles of milk in the box she carried. Her face froze. "Who are you? What are you doing here? Where's Venus and . . ."

"I'm Gus Brinkmeyer. Venus invited me." His voice came out quiet, sounding as meek as Mrs. Taylor's cat when she was just a kitten. "Can I help you with . . . ?"

"Venus!" the woman yelled, disappearing into the next room.

Gus figured this was Venus's mother, and she obviously wasn't happy to find him here.

CHAPTER 47

CHOCOLATE CAKE AND TOOTHBRUSHES

From his chair, Gus heard their voices. He couldn't make out many words, but he knew he wasn't welcome. He got up, folded the afghan, and fumbled for his socks. One had tumbled under the chair, and he got on his hands and knees to reach for it.

"What are you doing?" Venus stood over him with a tray of tea and chocolate cake.

Gus snapped to a sitting position. "I'm leaving. I didn't mean to make trouble with your mother."

"But you're here," she said. "And you can't cross the river. You have to stay."

"But—"

"No buts. My mom has to . . ." Venus stopped. "Just eat your cake and drink your tea."

Gus had finished the cake and was sipping the last of the tea when Mrs. Marlowe came back into the room.

"Mom is sorry for being rude, Gus," Venus said, but her mother didn't look sorry.

"I wouldn't have come," Gus said, "but I didn't know where else to go. The river—"

"The American Legion is providing shelter from the flood," Mrs. Marlowe said. "I can tell you where to find them."

"Mother!" Venus nearly shouted.

"Better for him to get there while they still have room."

"Look at him, Mom," Venus said, as though Gus weren't listening. "He's drenched, and his lips are blue. You can't send him back out in the rain like that. We can at least give him dry clothes before he goes to the Legion hall."

"I don't think your dresses will fit me," Gus said with a nervous laugh.

"Mom?" Venus raised her eyebrows.

Her mother shook her head. "We can't."

"We might have some clothes that would work," Venus said, raising her eyebrows again. "We wouldn't want Gus to end up with pneumonia or trench foot on our account."

"He'll just get wet again," Mrs. Marlowe said as Venus disappeared down a hall.

"I'm sorry to have caused all this trouble," Gus said.

Venus's mother said nothing.

Gus tried to fill the silence. "Venus gave me some of the chocolate cake she baked. It's really good."

"I suppose so," Mrs. Marlowe said. "Personally, I don't care for chocolate."

What? Hadn't Venus said it was her mother's favorite?

Venus returned with some folded items and handed

them to Gus. She lifted trousers from the pile and held them up. They were way too short. But they were dry!

"Do you have any . . . ?" Gus blushed. How could he ask Venus about *underwear*?

"There are underwear and socks, too," Venus said.

"Is there somewhere I can dry off and change?" Gus asked.

"Bathroom's the first door on the left." Venus pointed.

Gus stepped into the bathroom and closed the door. He felt like beating his head against the wall. *Stupid, stupid Gus.* Had he ever felt more embarrassed and foolish? And he had started a quarrel between Venus and her mother. He needed to dress quickly and be on his way.

He unfolded the garments and wondered whose they were. Were they left behind by Venus's father? He peeled off his wet clothes, heaped them on the floor, and shivered in his nakedness.

A fluffy, white towel hung from a hook. Gus dried his face and hair first, but stopped when he saw how grubby the pristine towel became. Sweating over the sandbags had left him filthy, and he still felt the grit of sand on his skin. He hadn't showered in nearly a week. This would not endear him to Venus's mother.

He reached for the bar of Ivory soap from the sink. He lathered himself up and rinsed off. He toweled himself dry, even between his toes. He avoided the open blisters on his heels, careful not to get blood on the white towel.

177

The borrowed clothes were not only too short, but too big around. Gus couldn't imagine the man who could wear trousers this size. But he had no complaints about dry clothes.

The wool socks were black, so at least the blood from his heels wouldn't show. His feet savored the warm socks for a few seconds before he slipped back into his wet shoes.

Whispers crept through the wall. Were Venus and her mother arguing again? Because of him? He sure had loused things up. But was it all *him*? Why did Venus say chocolate cake was her mother's favorite, and her mom said she didn't even like chocolate? It didn't make sense.

He tucked in the shirttails and looked in the mirror above the sink. He combed his hair as best he could with his fingers. He wouldn't be so bold as to use Venus's comb or hairbrush.

Bundling his still-wet trousers, socks, and underwear into a ball, Gus wrapped them inside his shirt and tied them with its sleeves. He took a last glance around the bathroom to make sure he hadn't left a stray sock.

Just as he reached for the doorknob, his eye caught the toothbrush holder hanging from the wall above the sink. It held *three* toothbrushes. *Three!* Who else kept a toothbrush here besides Venus and her mom?

CHAPTER 48

THREE FACES

Venus waited for Gus in the living room.

"Thanks," he said. "It's good to be dry." He didn't say how ridiculous he felt in the ill-fitting clothes. And he didn't ask the questions that begged for answers. *Why did you lie about chocolate cake? Whose clothes are these? Why do you have three toothbrushes?*

He did ask one question. "How do I get to the Legion hall?"

Venus took his hand. "I'm sorry you have to leave," she said, "but I've defied my mom enough for one day."

"Why don't you and your mom come with me?" Gus asked. "This flood is serious." He remembered Richie and his rowboat. "What if you need something from the store? How will you get it if the water goes higher?"

"We'll stay," Venus said emphatically.

"Why?" asked Gus. "I don't understand."

Venus answered. "We have to stay because . . ."

"The house," Mrs. Marlowe said as she came into the room. "We have to keep an eye on the house."

"What if the water rises all the way to your front door?"

"This house sits on a hill, much too high for that to happen. We'll be fine," Mrs. Marlowe told Gus. "Let me tell you how to get to the American Legion hall." She pointed. "Three and a half blocks east and turn right." Gus tried to imprint the directions in his mind when a noise came from a back room.

"What was that?" Gus asked. "Sounded like something fell."

"I left laundry on your bed, Venus," Mrs. Marlowe said. "It must have fallen. Run check, will you?"

The loud thump Gus had heard didn't sound like a noise laundry would make, but Venus scurried from the room.

He wanted to follow her, but Mrs. Marlowe blocked his path. "Do you have those directions straight?" she asked.

Gus nodded and slid his coat sleeves over the outsized shirt and buttoned it. Below the coat's hem, the short trousers left a glimpse of naked leg above the borrowed socks, even though Gus pulled the socks as high as they would go.

He grabbed his damp clothes as Mrs. Marlowe hurried him toward the front door. "Good luck to you," she said.

Hanging his soggy bundle of clothes on the Schwinn's handlebars, Gus walked the bicycle across the lawn to the street. Looking back at the house as he slid onto the seat, he saw faces watching him from between the Venetian blinds. *Three* faces!

The faces disappeared in a flash, but Gus had seen them. And he was sure of the number. Three faces to go with three toothbrushes. The unexplained male voice on the telephone? The noise from the back room? *Laundry, my foot!* Three people were in that house. But why would Venus and her mother lie about it?

Weird things were happening. Secret things. Gus tried to make sense of it.

Mrs. Marlowe was divorced. Did she have a boyfriend? One who was short and round? One who liked chocolate cake? One who lived here with them? She might want to keep something like that a secret. Oh, thunder! Wouldn't *that* rattle Aunt Mary's rosary beads?

CHAPTER 49

CRASH

Rain splattered Gus's face as he headed into the wind, pedaling Pete's Schwinn as fast as he could. His bundled clothes hung from the handlebars and thwacked against his knee each time he pumped. Water splashed behind the tires, and he felt it lash his bare legs between socks and trousers.

He didn't want to go to the Legion Hall. He wished there were a way to get across the river and go home. He still hadn't given Dad's message to Mom. It had been two days since he'd left Dad. Mom had to be worried. And what about Pete? Gus had treated him badly. Did Pete worry that Gus hadn't come home? Did he care?

Boyd Street was deserted. No cars. No people. Windows were dark. Even with rain and dreary skies, not one light. Except in Venus's house.

When Gus reached a cross street, he looked toward the river. *Holy smoke!* How had the water risen so high in one day? He glanced back toward Venus's house. Did they realize how near it was, how imminent the danger?

182

He had to warn them. He turned around to pedal back to the brown house. On the river side of the street, water encroached between homes. At a vacant lot, the water was close enough for him to make out floating tree branches, roof shingles, a mailbox. And something wrapped in a blanket. A *baby*?

Gus braked the bike so quickly, it skidded on the wet road, slipping, sliding, and wobbling uncontrollably. Gus struggled to keep the bike upright, but the weight of his wet clothes on the handlebars threw it off balance.

With a crash, the bicycle went down and careened along the pavement on its side. Gus's right foot tangled with the pedal. He felt fabric tear away from his skin, winced at the scrape and burn of his leg and thigh along the asphalt.

The front tire hit the curb and came to an abrupt stop. Pain shot through Gus's foot, but he pulled himself up and hobbled back to the vacant lot, to the edge of the water, dragging his injured foot behind him.

The blanketed object washed farther out into the water, where Gus couldn't reach it. He plunged toward it, ignoring the river's chill seeping through his clothes, failing to notice the way its current took hold of him. Knee-deep, he still wasn't able to reach the floating body. Waist-deep. He stretched out and snagged the edge of the blanket, holding it fast. But the blanket unfurled, and the being inside came loose and floated downriver!

CHAPTER 50

THE
AFGHAN

A *teddy bear! Just a toy!*

Relief surged through Gus—for a moment. But fear gripped him when he realized he was as helpless as the bear. The undertow knocked him off his feet, gripped his legs, and tried to drag him out into the river. He struggled to keep his head above water, while an unseen power, with the strength of an Ironton Tanks linebacker, pulled him beneath the surface.

But Gus wasn't a stuffed toy. He could fight. He pushed upward, grabbed a deep breath, and plowed toward the water's edge. The river tugged. Gus tugged harder. *Pull, Gus, pull,* he told himself, forcing his legs to move. Closer. Almost.

One last thrust toward land before Gus collapsed onto the ground. He lay unmoving, except for the heaving of his chest as he labored to catch his breath.

When water lapped at him again, he crawled further from its grip. He reached the curb and pulled himself to a sitting position. He looked for the bicycle, but it had moved. No. Gus had moved. The current had carried him past the vacant lot.

He limped to where the wrecked Schwinn lay in the street. Its fender was smashed and its front wheel bent. Spokes stuck out every which way. Pete would surely throttle him.

The whole right leg and seat of the borrowed trousers was torn clean through. The skin on his leg and thigh had lost a few layers as well. On his shin, a deeper gash, jagged like a bicycle chain, oozed blood. His right foot was the worst of it. When he tried to move it, pain pierced him like a dagger.

Rain continued to pelt him. Grappling his way out of the river had left him spent, but he was alive. He lay back on wet grass and looked up at the dreary gray sky, at gloomy clouds that never seemed to empty. He stared at those clouds until he closed his eyes against the sting of raindrops. He mumbled incoherently. Was he cursing the rain? Or the river? Maybe he was praying, thanking God for saving him from the flood. He wasn't sure. His mind jumbled with confusion. He couldn't stay here. He had to warn Venus about the flood. But he didn't have the strength to move.

~~~

Gus must have fallen asleep. Weird dreams took hold of him. He was jostled, lifted, and poked at. Voices buzzed in his ears, but no words reached his brain. It was like fighting the river again, but this time the water was inside his head.

185

Warmth eased into him, and he might have thought he'd died and gone to heaven, but pain kept him firmly rooted to Earth.

Opening his eyes was a struggle, but he managed to allow a slit of light to edge through his eyelashes. Someone leaned in and blocked the light.

Gus tried to focus on the face, a round face with an awkward smile. No one he recognized. Looking down from the face, he saw something he did recognize. A purple afghan.

CHAPTER 51

DAVID

"David!" The word came in a harsh whisper. "Come away from there."

"He'th alive." The male voice said the words slowly with a sort of lisp, almost as though his tongue were too big for his mouth.

Gus opened his eyes again. It was a boy.

"I know he's alive. You need to let him sleep." The whisper came from Venus, and it wasn't harsh anymore, but gentle.

Gus forced his eyes to open all the way, made his lips form a word. "Who?"

"He talkth like an owl," the round-faced boy said.

Gus gazed past the face to Venus. He was in her living room. He felt the cushioned back of a couch to his left, and his right foot, sticking out from under the purple afghan, was covered by an ice bag.

"How?" Gus said. "How did I get here?"

"Mom and I brought you," Venus said. "Your bicycle crashed just up the street. David saw you go down and told us."

"David?"

"Me," the boy said with a grin. "I'm twelve." He held up six fingers.

"Yes," Venus said. "David's my brother."

"You have a brother?" The third toothbrush. The third face in the window. The noise from the back room. "Why didn't you tell me?"

"That's not important. Mom thought your foot was broken at first. She went to fetch the doctor yesterday, but she couldn't get through because of the flood."

"Yesterday? How long have I been here? My foot's broken?"

"Mom thought so at first. Now she thinks it's just a bad sprain. You crashed your bicycle yesterday. I brought it here, but I don't think it's fixable. We thought it best to let you sleep. It's Saturday afternoon, and you must be hungry. Mom's making soup."

"Chicken thoup," David said.

Gus looked closer at David. He was shorter than Venus, but wider. A writer would have described him as *squat*. Short and round. Of course! The clothes Gus had borrowed were David's. They had to be. But Gus was no longer wearing wet clothes. He had on a dry shirt, or maybe a pajama top, but he didn't remember putting it on. "Who . . . ?"

"Go check on the soup, David," Venus said. "Tell Mom Gus is awake."

When David left the room, Venus said in a low voice, "Now you know our secret. We don't tell people about David. Sometimes they scare him, and sometimes they're mean. He's safer here away from prying eyes."

"You could've told *me*," Gus said.

"You know if it weren't for David," Venus went on, "you'd still be lying unconscious at the side of the road. Thank God you're all right."

"Thank God and David," Gus said, but he hardly felt "all right." His head ached, the side of his leg burned, and his foot throbbed with pain.

His hand crawled under the afghan toward his scraped leg and felt his bare skin. Someone had undressed him!

CHAPTER 52

ON THE COUCH

Gus felt a blush creep up his face. "Where . . . where are my clothes? And who . . . who?"

David came up behind Venus. "I told you he talkth like an owl."

"My mom treated your scrapes," Venus said, trying to hide a bit of her own blush. "She's a nurse."

Her mother had undressed him? Her mother who despised him for coming here?

"She had to cut off your trousers," Venus said.

"*My* trouthers," David said. "You tore 'em real bad."

"Sorry," Gus said. "I didn't mean to."

"You wrecked your bithycle," David said. "I thaw you."

"David likes to watch from the window," Venus explained.

"I thaw you go in the water," David said.

Venus looked at Gus. "You went in the river? Don't you know you could've contracted typhoid or cholera or some other horrible disease?"

190

"There was something wrapped in a blanket," Gus said. "I thought it was a baby, but it was a teddy bear." He felt like a sap for mistaking a toy for a baby. But something more than his foolishness niggled at his addled brain.

"You risked your life to rescue a baby," Venus said. She fumbled for his hand and squeezed his fingers.

"A teddy bear," Gus said, "and I didn't rescue it. It's still in the river." *The river!* That was it! "We all need to get out of here. The river's practically at your doorstep!" He almost jumped up from the couch, but remembered just in time that he was half naked beneath the purple afghan.

"The flood is across the street," Venus said. "Not at our doorstep. Our house sits on a rise, where the river can't reach. No flood ever has. Besides, you're in no shape to go anywhere."

Mrs. Marlowe brought a bowl of soup to Gus.

"Mom," Venus said. "Gus went into the river after he wrecked his bicycle."

"Is that true?" Venus's mother asked.

Gus nodded.

Mrs. Marlowe shooed Venus from the room. "I have to check his injuries," she said. "If you were in that dirty river, Lord knows what kind of germs seeped into your open skin."

As she pulled back the purple afghan, Gus turned his face away. Right now Venus's mother seeing his bare skin seemed a worse fate than any disease. He just might die from embarrassment.

191

"No need to be uncomfortable," she said. "I'm a nurse, I've been married, and I have a son. You don't have anything I haven't seen before."

Her words did nothing to chase away his uneasiness. He closed his eyes. He felt her fingers probe along his leg and thigh, all the way to his hip and backside. She touched lightly around the jagged gash on his shin.

"There's no redness around the wounds," she said. "No sign of infection." She pressed her hand to his forehead. "No fever either. I'll need to keep an eye on you though."

~ ~ ~

Gus lay on the Marlowe couch the rest of the day. David brought Gus a robe to wear, and Gus slipped his arms into its too-short sleeves. He made certain the robe covered him before he eased back the afghan. It took three tries and a sturdy grip on the arm of the couch for Gus to stand. Pain twisted through his arms and legs.

David looked up at him. "Guth can walk now?"

"I sure hope so," Gus said, holding back a grimace. He leaned on Venus and her mother to limp to the bathroom door. At least he was allowed privacy inside that small room. But he felt wobbly and didn't dawdle before stumbling back to the couch.

David seemed to feel Gus was his responsibility. He sat on a chair beside the couch and talked to him.

"Are you my friend, Guth?"

"I'd be happy to be your friend," Gus said, reaching out for David's stubby hand and shaking it.

"I never had a friend before," David said. He lowered his eyes. "I can't do thingth like other people. Never like Venuth."

"It's nothing to be ashamed of," Gus said. "I can't do a lot of things as well as my brother. And Pete's younger than I am. It's just the way it is."

Gus had never said those words out loud before. Pete was better at so many things. *It's just the way it is.*

"Venuth liketh me anyhow," David said. "Even though I can't do thingth. I bet your brother liketh you, too."

"Of course he does," Gus said, but his mind thought back to his fight with Pete the morning he and Dad had left to fill sandbags. And even before that. Ever since New Year's dinner when he'd blamed Pete for the uproar. Maybe Pete *didn't* like him so much anymore. Who could blame him?

Gus needed to make things right with Pete. And with Mom and Dad. He hadn't delivered Dad's message. He had let everyone down.

Maybe that's why he'd been spared from the flood. So he could set things straight at home. But he'd have to get there first.

CHAPTER 53

WATER AND ICE

Venus's mother regularly checked Gus for fever or redness. And found none. She changed the ice bag on his ankle. Her soothing voice almost made Gus forget the icy tone she'd used when she'd sent him out into the rain the day before.

"Venus fetched your wet clothes from your bicycle," Mrs. Marlowe said. "They're hanging in the kitchen and should be dry enough to wear by tomorrow."

"Tomorrow?" Gus said. "Are we safe here until tomorrow?"

"We're safe here as long as we need to be," Venus's mom told him. "The flood could rise another dozen feet, and we'd still be too high for it to reach."

Gus remembered the mound the Marlowe house sat on. She was probably right, and he tried not to think about the flood. But lying on a couch gave a fella lots of time to think, and the flood wasn't the only thing that troubled him.

He still needed to make things right at home.

~~~

On Sunday, Mrs. Marlowe helped pull Gus's trousers over his swollen foot, which nearly matched the color of the afghan.

"We'll have cold meals today," she told him, tucking the ice bag around his foot. "The power went out overnight, but there's still a sizable chunk of ice in the ice box, I can chip off enough for the ice bag."

"How will your refrigerator work without electricity?"

Mrs. Marlowe laughed. "Not a refrigerator. An ice box."

"Oh." Gus felt a bit foolish. Grandma Walsh used to have an old wooden ice box with a compartment for a huge block of ice. He hadn't realized some folks still used those.

"When I was a girl, our house didn't have electricity," Mrs. Marlowe continued. "We managed then. We'll manage now. But we'll have to manage without heat. With no power, the fan went out on the oil burner."

Before she left the room, Mrs. Marlowe draped a blanket around David's shoulders.

Gus limped to sit beside David at the window. He could see the river between houses across the street. He watched it lap at their foundations. It was closer than yesterday. He remembered its force when it had tried to drag him under. And he could still picture floodwater gushing against the sandbag wall.

He went back to the couch and asked Venus, "Can't you convince your mom to evacuate?"

"She won't," Venus said. "You don't understand how

it is for David. Mom used to take him places, but people stared. When David was four, some kid called him names and pushed him down. So we keep him home. I stay with him when Mom works, and she's here when I'm in school."

"I'm sorry," Gus said. "I would've liked to get my hands on the kid who pushed him."

Gus saw a smirk creep onto Venus's mouth. "*I* took care of it," she said. "I was only seven, and the kid was about nine, but I socked him in the stomach." She didn't look one bit sorry.

David came over to the couch and tugged on Gus's sleeve. "Come look," he said.

Gus hobbled back to the window. He and David watched floodwater creep higher on houses across the street.

"I'm glad we don't live over there," David said.

"What about the people who do?" Gus asked Venus. "What about your neighbors?"

Venus bit her lip. "This whole neighborhood was evacuated nearly a week ago. We're the only ones left."

Gus realized he hadn't seen another person since the first moment he rode Pete's bicycle down Boyd Street. The four of them were completely alone. Stranded in the flood.

How could he fix things with Pete and his parents if he couldn't get to them?

CHAPTER 54

ISLAND

O n Monday, the swelling in Gus's foot started to go down, but the pain throbbed whenever he moved. That didn't stop him from going to the window. He perched on the arm of the chair where David sat wrapped in a blanket.

"A waterfall," David said, pointing to floodwater that spilled over the curb on the other side of the street.

Water filled the street, and fear filled Gus. This flood was different from any he'd ever seen.

David turned to the large radio in the corner. He clicked the radio dial on and off repeatedly, but nothing happened.

"The power's off," Gus reminded him.

"It's time for *Flash Gordon*. You like *Flash Gordon*, Guth?"

"Maybe I could read you a story instead," Gus suggested. "Do you have any books?"

"Good idea," Venus said. "David loves 'The Owl and the Pussy-Cat.'"

Gus had stared at the flood all day, a flood he could do nothing about. Boyd Street resembled one of those Venice canals he had seen in pictures. Maybe reading to David was a way to push the rising water to the back of his mind. But the back of his mind was already filled with shame for the way he'd treated Pete. And regret for failing to tell Mom where Dad was. The flood wasn't his fault, but so much else was.

When he finished reading the poem, he watched muddy water creep through dead grass up the mound toward the front steps. He watched until dusk, when the flood was swallowed up by darkness. But the dark only hid what Gus knew was there.

Lying on the couch that night, shivering under his coat and the purple afghan, Gus was unable to sleep. It was cold and rain still pounded the roof overhead, but that wasn't what kept him awake. *I have to do something,* he thought. *But what?*

He wished Dad were here. Dad always seemed to have the answer. Or Pete. How would Pete handle this situation? He recalled when he, Pete, and Richie had called themselves the Three Musketeers. They had believed they could do anything as long as they did it together. He wished they were here right now.

~~~

On Tuesday morning, Gus woke to find David on a chair beside the couch. David tugged on Gus's arm. "Come look, Guth."

Gus limped behind David into the kitchen. David pointed out the window to a backyard covered with floodwater.

198

Hobbling back to the front window, Gus saw the water in the Marlowe front yard. The bottom step had disappeared, and the river sloshed against the second one. The brown house was like an island, surrounded by river on all sides. A river still rising. When would it stop? And what could prevent it from going all the way to the front door? And further?

Gus called to Venus and her mother. "It's getting deeper," he said. "I know you don't want David in a shelter, but maybe we could go to my house."

"How can we do that?" Venus asked. "There's no way to cross the river. Or even the street."

"There has to be a way," Gus said. "My friend Richie Weber said Coast Guard boats can cross the river." What Richie had actually said was *only* Coast Guard boats could cross because the current was swift and treacherous. And he'd said it five days ago. Were they still getting across?

"How do we find the Coast Guard?" Venus asked.

"We need to make them find *us*," Gus said. He scanned the room and spotted the purple afghan. "Do you have a few clothespins?"

After Venus brought him a handful of wood clothespins, Gus stepped out on the front stoop.

"Hey!" he called inside to Venus. "The rain stopped!"

Unlike other breaks in the storms, this time sun ventured out from behind the clouds. And the clouds were no longer dark ones. While Gus felt relieved to have nothing falling from the sky, what had already fallen swelled around the house, dashing muddy water against the steps.

Venus walked out to see the proof, holding her hand out from under the stoop's small roof. "Finally," she said.

"Without rain, we'll have a better chance of catching someone's eye with this." Gus tucked the afghan under his arm while he climbed onto the wood rail along the stoop.

"Be careful," Venus said. "Your ankle hasn't healed yet. You don't want to fall again."

The wood creaked under Gus's weight as he reached up to the gutter to attach the afghan with clothespins. When it fluttered from the roof, he climbed back down. The railing had felt unsteady beneath his feet, and the stoop didn't feel so solid anymore either. He could feel the river dashing against its supports. He hurried inside.

"Do you think someone will see it?" Venus asked.

"All we can do is hope and pray."

David sat by the window and recited some words over and over. He said them quickly and Gus didn't understand. David ran the words together like a song. That's it! He was singing. Or trying to.

It took Gus a minute to recognize the song, but he finally figured it out. "It Ain't Gonna Rain No More." Gus knew that song and sang along. David laughed, and they began again. And again. The flood made Gus feel helpless, but seeing the smile on David's face made him feel useful.

"Jeepers!" Venus said. "Enough."

"Enough rain," Gus said. "But never enough singing about it. Right, David?"

They began another chorus. David laughed more than sang, and Venus's smile almost made Gus forget about the rising water. Almost.

CHAPTER 55

THE
STOOP

When they tired of singing, Gus read "The Owl and the Pussy-Cat" again. He read it twice. Three times. When he put the book down, they began to sing again. He wasn't sure if he was trying to distract David or himself.

"Quiet, you two!" Venus said, putting her finger to her lips. "Do you hear that?"

Gus listened until he heard the sound, too. *Putt-putt-putt.*

"Look!" David said. "A boat!"

"A motorboat." Gus pointed. "On the next street." He rapped on the window with his knuckles.

David pounded on the pane beside him.

"They can't hear you clear over there," Venus said, "not over the sound of their motor."

Gus flung open the front door and waved both hands over his head. "Hey! We're here!" he called.

The boat kept moving.

He yanked the afghan from the gutter and waved it

202

over his head. The wood stoop swayed under his feet as the afghan flapped in his hands.

But the boat disappeared from sight.

"I don't think they saw you," Venus said.

Gus climbed to the railing and waved the afghan again, the rail creaking beneath his weight. As he stepped down to the stoop, a splintering sound filled his ears.

"Look out!" Venus yelled and pulled on Gus's arm.

The two of them leaped through the doorway, as the railing split right where Gus had just stood. It clattered onto the stoop.

"I'm so sorry," Gus said. But his apology was swallowed up by a loud crash.

A gush of water swept under the stoop and grabbed the steps leading up to it. Venus stood open-mouthed as her front steps floated away.

Water lapped against the house less than two feet below them. Gus pulled Venus back from the open doorway. He slammed the door just as the river snatched the supports from under the stoop and tore it off the house.

CHAPTER 56

RESCUED

David leaned his head against the windowpane. "It'th gone. It broke."

The river had become a predator, stalking them like a wild animal, trapping them inside the Marlowe house. And now it toyed with them the way Gus had witnessed Imogene toy with a mouse.

"Wait!" Gus held up his hand. He'd heard a sound. He listened again.

"Hey!" a voice flitted in the distance. "Hey!"

Gus opened the door. The *putt-putt* of the motor boat rumbled closer. "Here we are!" Gus yelled. "Over here!"

Two men sat in the boat, one skinny as a broom handle, the other plump as a prize hen. They cut the engine and idled right up to the door.

"We're from the American Legion," the skinny man said. "You folks look in need of aid. Climb aboard."

"Pea-green boat," David said, quoting "The Owl and the Pussy-Cat." "Pea-green boat."

The two men exchanged judgmental looks, and Gus watched Mrs. Marlowe grit her teeth.

The plump man gripped the doorsill to hold the boat steady as the other man reached his hand to Venus. Mrs. Marlowe helped David into the boat before she followed him. Gus brought up the rear, dropping carefully on his good foot.

"We likely wouldn't have come down this street," the heavy man said, "if we hadn't seen you waving that big purple flag. You folks are the only ones left down this way."

The skinny man pulled a cord a few times until the motor caught and started the *putt-putt* sound. Gus had never been in a motorboat before, and it was hard to believe this was the Ohio River, this waterway that stretched between buildings and seemed to cover every inch of land.

"This flood has shelters packed to the gills," the plump man said, "but we'll find a safe place for you somewhere."

"Can we go to the Ohio side of the river?" Gus asked.

"Impossible. Nobody can cross the river."

Gus tried again. "What about the Coast Guard?"

"Coast Guard cutters are for emergencies."

"My family doesn't know where I am," Gus said. "They expected me home a week ago, and the telephone's out so I can't call. My mom's got to be in a real lather by now. Is that enough of an emergency?"

The man rubbed his chin. "What do you think, Joe?" he asked his partner.

"I've been hoping for a reason to use that nifty, new-fangled talk-box the Coast Guard fellas left us," Joe said.

"Yeah," the other man said. "What they call that thing?"

"A walkie-talkie."

"We can call the Coast Guard from the Legion hall and see if they're willing to take you," he said. "But I wouldn't count my chickens yet if I were you. When they said 'emergency,' I'm sure they meant blood or broken bones."

"What about this?" Gus rolled up his trouser leg to show the jagged gash from the bicycle chain and his ankle puffing out over the top of his shoe.

"Mighty pretty shade of blue you got there," the man said.

~~~

With the boat tied to a street sign, the fat man waited with Gus and the others, while Joe climbed overboard into shallow water and waded toward the Legion hall.

When Joe returned, he scrambled back aboard. "Coast Guard will meet us down on Water Street." He laughed. "I reckon it's just water now, no street.

Gus looked at Venus. "Don't worry," he told her. "Way up on Fifth Street, my house will be as high and dry as Noah's Ark." At least it had been five days ago.

CHAPTER 57

CROSSING THE RIVER

The American Legion men handed off Gus and the Marlowes to the Coast Guard. "Something wrong with the kid?" asked one man. "He doesn't look right."

Gus bit back angry words. "The kid's just fine," he said. "The problem is mine." He rolled up his trouser leg.

"Is it broken?" the man asked. "Can you take off your shoe?"

"Not if I want to put it on again."

"Your leg doesn't look infected, but it's best to have a doctor give it a look. We can take you to Ashland or Ironton."

"Ironton," Gus insisted.

The Coast Guard cutter left the almost-tame water between buildings and headed out into the rushing flow of the river. The metal framework of the Ironton-Russell Bridge loomed above them, seeming near enough to touch as the boat passed beneath it. Five days ago, Gus had ridden Pete's bicycle across that bridge. By now, the bicycle was river debris.

Skimming crossways to the river's current was a mite like a horse jumping fence rails. Up. Down. Swoop. Plop. Gus's stomach lurched with each jolt. He gripped his belly and swallowed vomit, unwilling to let himself throw up in front of Venus, her family, and these men in uniform.

In the swiftly moving boat, the wind slapped sprays of icy water into Gus's face. His teeth chattered while his stomach rolled.

A man in uniform looked at Gus. "You jake?" he asked.

"No, I'm Gus."

The man laughed. "I meant are you feeling all right. You're a little green around the gills."

Gus made light of his nausea. "My ankle turned purple. Green's a step up." But his stomach didn't let him off the hook. The man plunked a bucket at Gus's feet just in time.

"Guth ith thick," David said. "Poor Guth."

"What about you, David?" Venus asked. "Do you feel sick?"

"No," David said. "Mom ith thick."

What? Mrs. Marlowe was sick, too? Gus looked up to see her leaned over her own bucket. He wasn't *happy* about Venus's mother, but maybe a speck relieved he wasn't the only one.

The Coast Guard officer said, "You should have seen it a few days ago. Raining pitchforks and the wind blowing up a gale. I think everybody was ready for sick bay."

Gus sat up and let the air brush his face. He gulped deep breaths and blew them out. His stomach settled.

On the Ohio side of the wide, wide river, the boat slowed. Gus didn't recognize this town, where roof peaks seemed to float on muddy water. Was this really Ironton? Above one of the roofs, a sign read *Lyric*. The Lyric Theater! On Second Street! Its sign barely visible above the flood. It was all so impossible.

"We can't go far inland," the officer said. "Too many things beneath the surface to snag on. We'll transfer you to a local rowboat. There's a couple fellas who navigate this stretch pretty regular. We'll track down one of them."

After a few minutes of inching along the river's edge, the officer shouted, "Ahoy! Ahoy in the rowboat!"

"Ahoy!" a voice answered from somewhere in the distance.

"Someone aboard needs medical attention," the officer called to the voice. "Can you take him to a doctor?"

"I sure can," came the reply. A familiar voice.

A small *thunk*. A bump against the cutter as another boat pulled alongside. A small boat. A rowboat. Gus looked over the side and into the face of Richie Weber!

CHAPTER 58

GOING HOME

"Richie Weber! You're a sight for sore eyes!" Gus called to his friend before Richie and the Coast Guard helped David and the ladies over the side of the cutter and into Richie's rowboat. The boat rocked from side to side as everyone boarded.

"Pea-green boat," David said, as he settled onto a seat.

Gus made hurried introductions. "David saved my life," he added.

"I can help you row, Richie," Gus offered, eager to let Venus see him as capable of *something*. In the past few days, she had seen him shivering, weak, bruised, unclothed, and sick as a junkyard hobo.

"I can manage . . ." Richie began before looking up into Gus's face. He must have seen the pleading look there. "One for all and all for one," he finished, using the Three Musketeers' saying.

Gus sat beside him and manned an oar. But his arms were weak. Not like Richie's. *Richie must be as strong as an ox,* he thought and tried to keep up with his friend. In spite of being sick on the Coast Guard boat. In spite of lying on Venus's couch for days. In spite of crashing Pete's bicycle and fighting the floodwaters to reach a teddy bear. He grimaced through the pain and rowed. He refused to let the flood win this battle.

"The current's got a mind of its own," Richie said. "It'll try to pull you in the wrong direction. And what is the right direction? Where you headed? Marting Hospital?"

"No," Gus said, "just take me home." The word tasted sweet as honey.

"Water's pretty deep up that way," Richie warned.

Gus couldn't believe it. "On Fifth Street? Horsefeathers!"

"Me and Pop are staying over the Five and Dime," Richie said. "Flood's up to the second floor there."

Gus tried to imagine the Five and Dime underwater. But he had seen the Lyric. He didn't doubt it.

When they rowed past the top of the Norway maple in front of the Brinkmeyer house, broken branches dangled in the water. One more tug of the current would drag them away.

"Dang, Richie!" Gus said. "How can this be possible?" The queasiness returned to his stomach.

"At least you still got a house," Richie said. "Ain't much left of ours."

"Oh, thunder!" Gus said. "I'm sorry, Richie."

"You want me to take you someplace else?" Richie asked.

"Kingsbury School is a shelter. They got cots and free food."

"No." Mrs. Marlowe said her first word since she'd gotten sick on the Coast Guard cutter. "No shelter. We didn't come all the way across the river to join the huddled masses."

Gus noticed the open window of Mom's bedroom. Why would they open the window in January?

"Helloooo!" Gus called. "Hello, Brinkmeyers!"

A window slid up next door, and Mr. Geswein's bald head leaned out. "That you, Al?"

"It's Gus, Mr. Geswein. Is my family all right?"

"Pete said to tell you he took your mom and the kids to your Aunt Mary's. Just a few hours ago. They left a coal oil stove inside for heat." *Heat?* Heat sounded good.

"You planning to evacuate?" Gus called to Mr. Geswein.

"Not us," the neighbor answered. "We'll be right as rain here. Oops, poor choice of words." He looked skyward. "No more rain, Lord. Please."

"I guess if they're staying, we can, too." Gus looked at Mrs. Marlowe. "If you're sure that's what you want."

Gus knew what *he* wanted. To be out of the river. To have Venus and her family safe from the flood. To be home again. Though he'd never seen home look like *this.* And he still needed to mend fences with his family. But that would have to wait.

CHAPTER 59

THE ROOF

"We've come this far," Mrs. Marlowe said. "This is where we'll stay for now." Her voice was calm, but firm. She hardly resembled the woman who had banished Gus into the rain not so long ago.

"Venus, do you think you can climb up the roof into that window?" Gus pointed.

"What about David?" Mrs. Marlowe asked.

"We can help him," Gus said. "But Venus should go first."

While Richie struggled to keep the rowboat steady, Venus stepped into Gus's linked hands. He and Mrs. Marlowe boosted her up until she could climb onto the shingles. Once on the roof, Venus leaned down to help her mother.

"I won't leave David," her mother said. "Help him first."

But the rocking of the boat unnerved David, and he had trouble standing to step into Gus's hands.

"I think you need to go up and help Venus lift him," Gus told Mrs. Marlowe.

"Come on, Mom," Venus said. "We can do this."

The woman reluctantly stepped into Gus's hands and leaned onto the porch roof, where Venus helped her the rest of the way.

When Mrs. Marlowe sat beside Venus on the shingled roof, she called to Gus, "Now what?"

"The two of you lie on your stomachs and reach down for David, while I help boost him from here."

Gus sat beside David on the bow seat. "I'm going to sit here and hold your legs, David, so you can stand up. I won't let go. I promise."

David teetered to a standing position. He shook his head. "I can't."

"Just try," Gus said. "Be brave. Like Flash Gordon."

"Brave like Flash?" David said.

"Just like Flash. I won't let you fall."

David's squat body quaked with fear, but Gus spoke to him calmly and gripped his legs. "Now reach your arms up high," Gus instructed. "High as you can reach."

When David raised his arms, Gus felt the trembling in his stubby legs. "You're doing fine, David," Gus said. "Just like Flash. Keep reaching."

He felt David's weight shift from his legs, and knew Venus and her mom had hold of him. But could they pull him to the roof without falling or losing their grip on him?

Gus lifted David's stubby legs. As soon as David's waist

cleared the eaves, Gus pushed from beneath. When Gus saw David's waggling feet disappear onto the roof, he sat down to catch his breath.

"They're all sitting up there," Richie said from his vantage point on the rower's seat.

"Take David inside through the open window," Gus called.

Gus couldn't see them, but Richie nodded to let him know they had done it.

"All right," Mrs. Marlowe's voice came from the roof. "It's your turn, Gus."

"Thanks for everything, Richie. The Three Musketeers will be together again after this fool flood goes down."

"I'm not so sure," Richie said. "Pop's talking about moving away from Ironton after the flood. But don't say anything to Pete until we know for sure. He won't take it too well."

Gus noticed the crestfallen look on Richie's face. "Don't give up the ship yet, Richie," he said. "Your dad could change his mind."

While Richie struggled to control the rocking of the boat, Gus struggled to stand. His legs quaked. His bicycle crash, getting sick on the Coast Guard cutter, and trying to hold his own with rowing had left him as weak as the drooping branches of the Norway maple.

He took a deep breath. The edge of the roof was above

his knees. He put his weight on his good foot. All he needed to do was swing his other foot onto the roof and pull himself up. He tried, but his foot fell far short, and the pain in it was rekindled. Gus ignored the throbbing and swung his foot again. It was no use. Maybe he could heft his weight onto the roof with his arms. Who was he kidding? He had to admit defeat. Sometimes, a person needed to swallow his pride and ask for help.

CHAPTER 60

A MUSKETEER

Mrs. Marlowe reached out her hands. "I'll pull you up."

"You aren't strong enough," Gus said.

Venus stood in the window. "I'll help."

"No," Gus said. "Stay with David."

Richie moved to the bow seat. "Stand on my shoulders," he told Gus.

Gus put his good foot on Richie's shoulder and pushed off. With one shove, Gus was on the roof beside Venus's mother.

He looked over the edge of the roof. "Thanks, Richie. You all right?"

"Fine as a flea's eyelash," Richie said. "You all keep safe. And keep an eye on Pete for me." He gave them a wave before he manned the oars again.

"You be safe, too," Gus called as he watched Richie row away. Such a good friend.

Actually, Richie and *Pete* had been best friends since they were little squirts, but they always made room for Gus.

It was Gus who'd named them the Three Musketeers. But Richie pronounced it Mus-KEE-ters. They'd dressed that way for Halloween once.

Gus chuckled at the memory. Richie, Pete, and Gus. Three best friends. Sometimes, it was hard to think of a brother as a friend, but Pete was surely both. Gus hadn't treated Pete like a friend lately. He had to correct that.

But he had more pressing concerns at the moment. He followed Mrs. Marlowe through Mom's bedroom window and closed it behind him.

Rubbing his hands together, Gus said, "I'll find that stove Mr. Geswein talked about." He left the others sitting on Mom's bed, while he went down the hall to the stairs.

The stairs he'd walked down nearly every day of his life now reached into the river. Gus looked over the banister. The sofa floated in muddy water, soggy and stained, and the bookcase poked its top shelf above murky water. Not a book in sight. Had someone taken them to safety before the water rose?

A memory from a couple weeks ago jolted back. Gus had been sitting at the dining table writing a poem to Venus when Timmy had traipsed into the room. Gus had slid the poem inside his book of Shakespeare plays. His cherished book. But he hadn't taken the book upstairs because Pete was there. He had shoved it behind the bookcase, the same bookcase now engulfed in floodwater.

How could a flood like this happen? Here? Gus had

grappled with a shovel and sandbags to protect other people's property. And he'd failed. But who could have predicted his own house, and his own property, would also fall victim to the same flood?

A sound from upstairs ended his self-pity. His book was not the only victim of this flood. Venus and her family were here. He needed to take care of them.

Going up the hall, he paused in the doorway of Timmy and Etta's room. "Come into this room," he called to the Marlowes. "There's a stove and jars of food."

The room was no warmer than outside, but they settled in chairs around the stove. Gus found matches on Etta's dresser, but he didn't know how to light the coal oil stove.

He brought blankets from the linen closet and scanned Etta and Timmy's room. Obviously, the family had been living up here. Oil lamps were lined up on Etta's dresser, next to the flashlight Dad always kept in the Buick for emergencies. Gus was the one who had taken it from the Buick's back seat the day Mr. Feldman gave him a ride from the American Legion hall.

"At least we have food," Gus said.

"Potty," David said, his knees clenched together.

"What about a bathroom?" Venus asked.

How had Gus not thought of that necessity? He wasn't used to being in charge. Dad always took care of everything. Gus was the one who let folks down.

CHAPTER 61

WATER AND HEAT

"Let me check," Gus said, and hurried down the hall to the bathroom.

Water in the toilet bowl looked as though it had flowed straight from the river. Beside the toilet sat a bucket of the same dirty water. Of course. It was for flushing the toilet.

He turned the hot-water faucet, but no water came from the tap. He tried the cold. Nothing.

A quart jug filled with water sat on the toilet tank. It looked clean. He opened the lid and took a sniff. It smelled clean.

Going back to the others, he said, "The bathroom is the first door on the left. The faucet doesn't work, but clean water's in a jug on the toilet tank. You can flush the toilet with river water. It's in a bucket."

"Come on, David." Mrs. Marlowe led her son to the bathroom.

When David and his mother returned, Gus edged down the stairs, holding tightly to the banister as he filled another bucket with floodwater to set in the bathroom. He wondered who had come up with the bucket idea. Dad or Pete? He remembered Dad's words that day at the American Legion hall. *Pete can handle things as well as I can.* The idea could have come from either of them. When it came to sensible things, Pete was head, shoulders, and cowlick above Gus. For some reason, the words didn't rankle as much as they had last week.

David smiled his crooked smile at Gus. So many things were more important than who knew about plumbing and who was a master of tools. Gus might not have handled things as well as Dad or Pete, but he'd managed to get Venus and her family to safety. They were safe here, right?

Venus took her turn in the bathroom next.

Gus wished Pete were here to light the coal oil stove. He checked to make sure it had plenty of oil. He held a match to the valve opening, but nothing happened. The flame didn't catch.

He asked Venus's mother, "You ever use one of these? Why won't it light?"

"Maybe if you hold down that switch while you light it."

It worked. She was right.

Venus appeared in the doorway. "I tried to turn on the bathroom light when I was in there, but either the bulb is burnt out or the electricity is off."

Gus flipped the switch on a lamp. "No electricity," he said. "I guess it was inevitable with the water so high."

Striking a match to an oil lamp's wick, he watched it sputter to life.

The light glinted off jugs of clean water lined up on the dresser with the jars of food. Gus would put another in the bathroom for washing up. Someone had thought ahead. Pete again?

Gus looked through the jars of food. "What should we have for supper?" he asked. "Green beans, okra, or carrots?"

David parked himself in front of the Brinkmeyer radio. "Flash Gordon," he said.

"No power," Mrs. Marlowe reminded him.

Gus looked at this boy who had spent his whole life sitting at the window or by the radio. Thank God he'd been at the window the day Gus had crashed Pete's bicycle. Gus might have brought Venus's family through a flood, but he owed her family a debt he could never repay.

CHAPTER 62

THE BOOK

After a cold supper of green beans and okra, Gus let Venus and her family take over the two front bedrooms.

It had been a long day, and he finally ambled to his own room. It looked surprisingly normal, except for some of the dining room chairs against the wall. And the mantel clock on the dresser. It still had the right time. Beside the clock was his book of Shakespeare plays. And his poem was still tucked inside the cover. Someone had rescued the book from behind the bookcase!

Pete? It must have been Pete. Gus clutched the book to his chest before stroking the embossed gold letters on its cover. Good old Pete had saved his prized book as well as Mom's clock. Like Richie, Pete had been a good musketeer. *One for all, and all for one.*

As Gus tugged his shoe from his swollen foot, he thought of his life like separate acts of a play. Mom, Dad, Pete, Etta, and Timmy were one act. Venus and her family were another.

And Richie? He supposed Richie and Pete were a different act.

He peeled off his filthy socks and slipped out of the dirty clothes he had worn and re-worn for more than a week. He thought of characters in Shakespeare's plays. Most characters didn't appear in only one act. They were part of the whole play.

He grabbed clean pajamas from his drawer and sped across the hall to the bathroom. There was no way to take a shower, but it would feel good to wash up. He dampened a washcloth and wiped his face and neck.

Easing around the gash on his shin, he washed all over with Mom's bar of Camay. He rinsed himself with the washcloth, using the jug's water sparingly. He scrubbed his feet carefully. His blisters had healed, but his swollen ankle throbbed like the dickens. He looked in the mirror and felt clean. Outside and in.

He put on two pairs of socks to keep his feet warm before crawling into his own bed for the first time in ten days. His sheets were like Arctic glaciers. He snuggled under his blankets and spread, pulling them all the way over his nose. He curled up and shivered while he waited to get warm.

He wondered about Venus and her family in the other two bedrooms. Were they warm enough?

Gus replayed the day in his mind, ending with finding his prized book. And the poem inside. He sat up as a thought struck him. If Pete had brought the book upstairs, had he read the poem? If he had, Gus was never going to hear the end of this. Pete would tease him without mercy.

But better Pete than Mom. What if Mom had found his book?

Tired as Gus was, nodding off was impossible. His private words to Venus had been exposed. And the girl he was stuck on like gum on the sidewalk, the one he had been forbidden to see, was sleeping in Mom and Dad's bed.

What would happen when all the acts of his "play" collided?

CHAPTER 63

A DAY ON FIFTH STREET

The sound of a toilet flushing woke Gus. Daylight eased through the window of his room. His room! He was home!

Throwing off the covers, he dressed in a hurry, trying to ignore the chill of his clothes against his skin. He slid two sweaters over his head.

In his stocking feet, Gus stood at the top of the flooded stairs. Was the water higher than it had been the night before? He wasn't sure. The Gesweins had chosen to stay. Was that wise?

In Timmy and Etta's room, David greeted Gus with a grin. Gus had moved this family once. He would keep the flood concerns to himself.

Jars of food were lined up on Timmy's dresser, but breakfast choices were limited. Three eggs sat in a bowl, but the small stove provided no surface to cook them on.

The hand-painted cookie tin was nestled among the jars of food. Gus looked inside. A handful of gingersnaps lay at the bottom. He passed them around. He found a jar of strawberry preserves, but there was no bread or biscuits to spread it on.

Venus passed out spoons she found in a dishpan. "We can pass around the jam and each take a bite."

"When you're hard pressed, press hard," Mrs. Marlowe said. "That's what my mother used to say."

They sat wrapped in blankets all day, trying not to shiver, but the chill seeped through the blankets.

"Hey, Guth," David said. "Rain no more?"

They all broke into singing "Ain't Gonna Rain No More" until David couldn't sing for laughing. It wasn't raining, but the floodwater wasn't receding either. Gus couldn't laugh, but he forced a smile to his lips. He would keep the worry inside.

"Pea-green boat?" David said.

"'The Owl and the Pussy-Cat'?" Gus said. "We didn't bring the book. And I don't know it by heart. Maybe I can tell you a different story."

Gus used to write gangster stories for Pete, but those didn't seem right for David. He reached for the cookie tin. Its peeling paint flaked in his hands.

"How about I tell you the story of this lovely family treasure?" Gus said. "Once upon a time, there was an old cookie jar, made of china and hand-detailed by artisans of the famed Sears, Roebuck establishment. It was filled with baked delights from the oven of Lady Ruth Brinkmeyer.

One day, only a single cookie remained. The two Brinkmeyer brothers both coveted that last tasty morsel. A fight ensued. In the scramble, the cookie jar met an untimely demise on the Brinkmeyer kitchen floor."

"No!" Venus said. "You and Pete fought over a cookie?"

If she only knew the things he and Pete had fought over.

"The two brothers felt awful," Gus went on. "And Lady Ruth was—shall we say, *less than pleased.* The brothers couldn't scrape up enough simoleons to buy a new cookie jar, so the younger brother painted an empty saltine tin. The older brother—the artisan—decorated it with the lovely strokes you see today."

Venus laughed. "And the older brother even spelled it correctly." Her smile rallied strength in Gus. Maybe he couldn't defeat the flood, but he could keep Venus and her family from thinking about it.

"Another thtory," David said.

Gus went on to tell adventures of the Three Mus-KEE-ters. He made up details, but the good times he had shared with Pete and Richie were genuine.

When Gus told the others, "Good night," and padded down the hall by the beam of Dad's flashlight, he stopped at the top of the stairs and shined the light down to the water. The rising water seemed to scoff at him. Telling stories had solved nothing.

CHAPTER 64

PETE

Thoughts swam in Gus's head as he tried to sleep. According to Mr. Geswein, his family was safe at Aunt Mary's. He'd thought being home would make him feel better, but this flooded house wasn't *home*. Not without Mom, Dad, Pete, and the little ones.

And he wasn't convinced they were safe here. Sleeping in his own bed didn't help. He didn't sleep any better than on the Legion hall floor, in the rowboat, or in the toolshed.

He finally got up and dressed. He flipped through the pages of his Shakespeare book. Tragedies. He didn't need to read a tragedy. He was living one. He unfolded his poem to Venus. What a silly, lovesick drip he'd been when he'd written those words.

Some day, he'd write a poem about the real Venus he had come to know. The girl who'd searched for him in the rain and found him in a toolshed. The girl who'd defied her mother and taken him home. The girl who'd punched a kid in the stomach to defend her brother.

When he heard the others moving around, he hurried past the top of the stairs to join them in Etta and Timmy's room. He had brought this family here. They were his responsibility. If that meant keeping their minds off rising waters, so be it.

"There's more jelly here," Venus said, "but I'm hungry enough to eat one of these eggs raw." She reached for a bowl. "Do I dare?"

She cracked the egg on the rim of the bowl and laughed. "They're hardboiled!" she squealed. "Hardboiled."

She reached a knife from the dishpan and carefully split two eggs in half. Each person got a half before she split the third egg into four pieces.

"Even steven," Gus said. But he noticed Venus's mother slipped her share to David.

After breakfast, Gus began another story about the Three Mus-KEE-ters. Richie the Lionheart, who bravely rescued folks in need. Sir Pete the Master-of-Tools, who could fix anything. And Lord Gus the Teller-of-Stories. He didn't mention the Gus whose job was to keep worry at bay.

At a climactic point in the story, they were startled by a noise from outside. It sounded as if someone was on the roof.

Tap, tap, tap! Someone *was* on the roof!

Gus slid open the window.

"It's Sir Pete," Venus said as Pete stepped inside.

"Thank God you're all right!" Pete said.

Hugging was something the brothers hadn't done since

they were little, but Gus threw his arms around Pete. And Pete maybe even hugged him back.

"The whole town's looking for you," Pete said. "Mom's half out of her mind with worry. We're all staying at Aunt Mary's."

Pete finally seemed to notice the other people in the room.

"Sir Pete." Venus bowed her head.

"What?" Pete looked dazed.

Venus and Gus laughed, and David said, "Mathter of Toolth."

"Venus's mom and her brother, David," Gus said.

Pete nodded his head in greeting and turned to his brother. "Where the dickens you been?"

"Toolshed, Venus's house, and—oh yeah—in the river. Nice get-up, Pete. Knickers are a fetching look for you."

"Don't let him tease you, Pete," Venus said. "You should've seen *him* a few days ago."

"I need to change while I'm here," Pete said. "You wouldn't believe the places I've been in this outfit. Even the courthouse."

"So are you here just to change clothes?" Gus asked. This was his chance to begin making amends.

"No," Pete answered. "I came to find you. I figured you went to Venus's, but when I couldn't cross the river, I pinned down Richie Weber. Didn't you see the note we left?"

Gus shook his head. "What note?"

Pete led him into Mom's room, where a slip of paper

peeked out from under a lamp. Pete handed it to Gus.

Bold letters declared, *We're safe at Aunt Mary's.* A hurried scrawl beneath it said, *I'm sorry, Gus. Don't be mad anymore.* It was signed, *Pete.*

Gus hugged Pete again. "I'm sorry, too. I'm sorry for so many things. How did you know I was at Venus's?"

"I knew you'd go to find her. But I didn't tell a soul. I swear."

"I believe you. You've always been a good brother. I'm sorry I let things come between us."

"You mean Venus?"

"I mostly meant I get bothered that Dad always prefers to do things with you instead of me. He seems to like you better."

"That's crazy," Pete said. "Dad loves you. He has no interest in poetry, and he doesn't understand Shakespeare, but he's proud of how smart you are. Sometimes he feels you're so smart he doesn't have anything in common with you."

"Are you sure?" Gus had never imagined Dad might feel intimidated by him.

"Of course I am. He and I work together. I hear the things he says about you. He tells me all the time that knowing how to use tools is the only way I'll amount to anything. But your brains will take you straight to the top."

Gus clapped Pete on the back. "We're both going places."

CHAPTER 65

AT AUNT MARY'S

"The place we need to go right now is Aunt Mary's," Pete said. "Mom and Dad are worried sick about you."

"Tell them I'm fine," Gus said.

"Tell them yourself. I doubt you'll get much of a tongue-lashing for disappearing without a word. The minute Mom sees you alive and breathing, all will be forgiven."

"You can tell her I'm alive and breathing."

"No," Pete said. "*You* need to do that."

"But what about Venus's family?"

"I guess they should come with us," Pete said. "If I show up without you, Mom will come here herself, even if she has to swim."

"But you know how Mom and Dad feel about . . . ," Gus whispered, "Venus."

Pete lowered his own voice to a whisper. "If you're going to keep seeing her, you'll have to face them sooner or later. They're less likely to lay into you with a bunch of people around." Pete laughed. "Heck, with all the people at Aunt Mary's, they might not even notice they're there."

Pete added, "The river crested yesterday. When the water goes down, there won't be any way out of this house except to wade through God-knows-how-much mud and silt. I brought a rowboat, and we should all leave now, while we can."

"One word of warning though," Pete added, "Aunt Mary will likely make all of them get typhoid shots."

~~~

Mom dang-near hugged the stuffing out of Gus. "Your dad said you were coming home with Mr. Feldman last week," she said. "Why didn't you?"

"I needed to check on Venus and her family," Gus said. "You had Pete to look after you and the kids, but Venus doesn't have a dad to do that. I wanted to help, but they ended up being the ones who helped *me*. I wrecked Pete's bicycle and was unconscious in the street, and—"

"You wrecked my bicycle?" Pete said.

"You were unconscious?" Mom said.

"And Venus's family rescued me," Gus went on. "They fed me and . . ." He blushed a bit. "Mrs. Marlowe tended my injuries."

"Injuries?" Mom's voice rose.

"He got scraped up when the bicycle went down," Venus's mother said. "But there's no infection, even though he was in that filthy floodwater."

234

"In the floodwater?" Mom's voice rose a bit more. "Dear Lord, what happened?"

Gus ducked aside to avoid another embarrassing hug.

"He saw what he thought was a baby," Venus said. "He went in the water to rescue it. With no thought for his own safety."

"You rescued a baby?" Pete asked. His eyes widened and his mouth stayed open.

"It turned out to be a teddy bear," Gus said.

"But Gus didn't know that," Venus defended.

"I s'pose that bear was mighty grateful," Pete teased.

"There's a lot to be grateful for," Mom said.

"And we're grateful to you," Dad said to Venus's mother. "It sounds as though we might have lost our Gus if not for you."

He turned and called out, "Hey, Mary, throw a little more water in the pot for tonight's supper. We have more mouths to feed."

So far, Mom and Dad were being especially nice to Venus and her family. But Gus saw the way they looked at him. He knew he was in trouble, and when there weren't so many people around, he was going to have to atone for his sins.

CHAPTER 66

ON THE STEPS

While Gus enjoyed the delay in whatever punishment awaited him, he was stunned by how Aunt Mary took to David. She doted on the boy, making sure he had plenty to eat and even giving up her bed for David and his mother. Aunt Maggie didn't look happy about being put out of a bed, but she didn't grumble out loud. Imogene took to sleeping at David's feet, and Aunt Mary didn't even complain about a cat in her bed.

At night, Aunt Mary's floors were jammed with people. Getting up to go to the bathroom was like maneuvering through an obstacle course.

Not only was Aunt Mary's house warm, but—filled with people—it was uncomfortably so. In the morning, Gus stepped to the front porch to get out of the oppressive closeness.

The chill felt almost good, but the flood smell hung in the air, a dank, damp stench Gus hadn't noticed before.

But he decided the flood stink was better than the crowded house.

Sitting on the porch steps, he heard the door behind him. Venus sat beside him and reached for his hand.

Gus squeezed her fingers. "It's been quite a week, hasn't it?"

"Definitely," she said. "Mom kept David in our house for eight years. And now he's come all the way across the river. She thought people would be mean to him. But your family's so nice."

"Some folks are scared by anybody who's . . . who's different," Gus said. "They just don't know how to behave toward someone who isn't the same as they are."

"My father sure didn't," Venus said, with a tinge of hurt in her voice. "When David was born, the doctor told Mom to put him in an asylum and forget he'd been born. Dad agreed with the doctor, but Mom refused. So Dad up and left."

"I'm sorry," Gus said.

"Dad's the one who lost out," Venus said. "Maybe if he'd stayed and gotten to know his son, he'd love him as much as me and Mom do."

"I think my aunt likes him, too," Gus said.

"You know what she told my mom?" Venus said. "She said, when her husband left for the war, she was expecting a baby. But the baby was born dead. The baby was . . . like David."

"I didn't know that," Gus said. "I knew her husband didn't make it to the war because he got the flu and died, but she never talks about him—or those days."

"You think her baby is the reason she likes David so much?"

"Could be," Gus said. With just a hint of a smile, he added, "It doesn't hurt that he has a name from the Bible."

Venus grinned. "Or does he have the name of a statue by Michelangelo?"

They laughed.

"I hope you meant what you said last week about still wanting to keep company with me," Gus said.

She looked down at their clasped hands, and peeped up at him through her blonde eyelashes. "I liked you from the moment I met you at the football game," she said. "And that was before I knew you would change my life."

Gus's jaw dropped. "I changed your life?"

"Mine, my mom's, and David's," she said. "You might have even *saved* our lives. I don't know how much water is in my house right now, but without you, we'd likely still be there."

Gus looked over his shoulder to the door. Seeing no one, he leaned toward Venus and kissed her.

CHAPTER 67

CLEANUP

After that first, crowded night at Aunt Mary's, the mighty Ohio began to recede. The water went down quickly as though someone had pulled out a giant bathtub stopper.

In its wake, the flood left behind a layer of muddy silt and a disgusting smell. It settled on streets and lawns. It clung to trees and houses. From parts of Seventh Street all the way to the riverbank, the grime and stink were everywhere.

Gus, Pete, and Dad spent day after day at the house on Fifth Street, mucking out the basement and the furnace, shoveling and sweeping mud from the floors, scrubbing and cleaning walls and furniture, hauling ruined things to the dump. Gus's hands wore calluses where they'd worn blisters less than two weeks ago.

The flood stink couldn't be washed off the refrigerator. Water had seeped into its insulation.

"We might be able to have the insulation replaced," Dad said. "But the motor must be ruined."

239

Pete disappeared upstairs and returned with something wrapped in a greasy towel. "I took the motor upstairs," he said.

Dad beamed and clapped Pete on the back.

"Only you would have thought of that," Gus said. *And only you would have known how to do it.*

~~~

Once the house was clean, Dad inspected the electrical wiring and made a list of what needed to be replaced.

Mom washed all the sheets, blankets, and clothes, which flapped on the clothesline while Gus and Pete started cleaning the garage.

"Everything is covered with that muddy muck," Pete said. "The wagon is filled with it. And look at your bicycle." He glared at Gus. "At least you still have a bicycle."

"I'll hose it down later," Gus said, "and fix the tire. Then you can have it."

The line of mud and silt by the garage windows showed how high the flood had reached. Pete climbed to the top of a stepladder and reached a sudsy sponge toward the gritty, slimy remains of the worst flood in Ironton's recorded history.

"Wait!" Gus said. "Before we wash it off, we ought to mark it somehow. For history. To show how enormous this flood was."

Pete shot his brother a smirk. "Or we could write a poem," he said in a smart-aleck tone. Making kissing noises from the top of the ladder, Pete said in a simpering voice, "Venus, my everlasting love."

Gus threw a scrub brush at Pete. "I knew you'd read it, you louse!" He gripped the legs of the stepladder and wobbled it.

"Knock it off," Pete said.

"Wait a minute," Gus said. "A poem's not a bad idea." Words were already forming in his head. He shot into the house to grab a pencil and paper.

"Hey!" Pete yelled after him. "You have to finish cleaning the garage!"

"Don't make your brother do all the work," Mom said when Gus reached the kitchen. "And don't think your dad and I are going to let you off easy for disobeying us."

Gus had known it was coming. It was time to face the music.

CHAPTER 68

WORDS

Now that Mom had brought up the subject, Gus wanted to get in his words first. "I'm sorry for leaving without telling you," he said. "And sorry I didn't let you know where Dad was. It was wrong. But it wasn't wrong to help Venus's family. They needed me."

"I know that," Mom said, "and Venus and her family seem nice. But if you want to keep seeing her, you're going to have to be honest with us from now on."

"I can keep seeing her?" Gus couldn't believe it.

"For now. But we expect you to see other girls, too. Catholic girls. You're too young to tie yourself down to one girl. Agreed?"

"Agreed," Gus said. He would have agreed to anything. Sometimes it took a tragedy to see what was important. And Gus realized how important his family was to him.

"And as punishment for disobeying us, I expect you to help get Etta caught up in her schoolwork."

"I promise," he said, knowing that it would truly be

a punishment. Etta was not easy to work with. She was probably even more stubborn than he was. But he was going to be able to see Venus.

He carried a pad of paper outside, where Pete sat atop the stepladder with his arms crossed impatiently.

"I'm not gonna clean this by myself," Pete said.

"Guess what," Gus said. "Mom said I can keep seeing Venus."

"I guess she figured you were going to anyway. This way, you'll see her on *their* terms."

"That's true. Now let's write that poem." Leaning against the stepladder, he wrote a line. *When the Ohio River rose.*

Pete read over his shoulder. "Say '*mighty* Ohio'," Pete suggested.

"The meter has to scan," Gus said, even though he knew Pete had no idea how poetic meter worked.

"I'm the one who suggested a poem," Pete said. "I think it needs to say 'mighty.'"

Gus changed the line. *When the mighty river rose.*

"Yeah," Pete said. "I like it."

Gus made scansion marks at the top of the page and wrote another line. *In '37, woe of woes.*

"Woe of woes?" Pete said. "What on earth does that mean?"

"It's a poetic way of saying it was the worst," Gus said.

"And how!" Pete agreed.

Pete grabbed a board leaning against the garage and

washed it with the sudsy sponge. "We can write it in paint on this, but the sign needs to explain that it marks how high the water was."

"We should have told Dad to get paint from the store," Gus said as he wrote another line.

Pete fetched a hammer and nail. "I'll pound a nail to mark where the silt line is. We can make the sign and hang it after we finish cleaning. We'll get paint on our way back to Aunt Mary's. I suppose we'll be ready to move home in a few days. I bet Aunt Mary is tired of riding herd on Etta and Timmy."

"Mrs. Marlowe's there, too. With David and Venus." Gus said. "You think she's tired of *them*, too?"

"I'm sure she's fed up with being the Good Samaritan and having a crowd underfoot," Pete said. "They're all impressed with the way you've kept the little ones in line with your stories every night."

Gus had liked doing that. The Three Mus-KEE-ters had become a nightly staple at Aunt Mary's.

"I know I'm ready to sleep in my own bed again," Pete said. "I never knew how much I'd miss clean sheets."

"Me either." Gus thought about the Legion hall floor, the rowboat, and the toolshed. He remembered lying half naked on Venus's couch.

"I'm even ready to go back to school," Pete said.

"I'm going to take a couple more days off to help clean Venus's house in Russell," Gus said. "I could use your help.

Her front steps and stoop need to be rebuilt. You know I'm no good at that."

"I'll say. But if I do that, you need to help me study for my algebra exam. And I think I'll help Richie and his dad. As close to the river as their place is, I'll bet it's even worse than our house."

Gus remembered his conversation with Richie. Obviously, Pete didn't know how bad Richie's place was. And Richie hadn't told him yet about possibly moving away.

CHAPTER 69

AFTER THE FLOOD

On Tuesday, February 9, Pete nailed the sign to the garage siding. Gus made sure Pete lined up the bottom of the sign with the nail hole he'd made before they scrubbed down the garage.

> *When the mighty river rose*
> *In '37, woe of woes,*
> *Everything below this sign*
> *Was underneath the waterline.*

Beneath those words, Gus had printed the names *Gus and Pete Brinkmeyer.*

"You put my name, too?" Pete asked. "*You* wrote the poem."

"But *mighty* was your idea," Gus said, "and so was writing a poem in the first place.

"I was just trying to get your goat." Pete climbed down from the ladder. "I didn't think you'd really write one."

246

"Maybe I should have put *Petey* on the sign," Gus said.

Pete smirked and raised the hammer.

Gus stepped back a step. "Don't do anything you'll have to confess to Father Gloekner next week."

Pete put the hammer in the toolbox. "It feels strange not to have been to Mass or confession in nearly a month. Dad said Saint Joe's is going to be torn down because of flood damage. I can't imagine it not being there."

"I know," Gus said. "Father Gloekner will say Ash Wednesday Mass in the school gymnasium tomorrow. What could be stranger than going to church at school?"

"I can think of all kinds of things that are stranger," Pete said. "Like Mom and Dad letting you have a Protestant girlfriend. And you being a hero who rescued a family."

"I'm not a—"

A whistle split the air, and the brothers looked toward the street, where Richie Weber stood, two fingers in his mouth, ready to let go another whistle.

Pete trotted out to meet Richie.

Gus stood by the garage and watched the two of them talk. He couldn't hear what they said, but Richie's serious face told him what he needed to know. Richie cracked his knuckles nonstop. Soon, Pete's face copied Richie's, and they both looked as if they'd been ordered to the principal's office. Pete put his hand on Richie's shoulder and Richie stared at the ground.

When Pete came back to the garage, he avoided Gus's

gaze. His eyes glistened. Tears? Pete was not the kind who cried.

Gus didn't let on what he already knew. "What's eating you and Richie?"

"The flood destroyed Richie's house." Pete looked at the ground just as Richie had. "They tore it down. With the liquor store gone, his dad is out of a job. And now out of a house."

"You know they'll rebuild the liquor store," Gus said.

"Maybe. But Richie's dad isn't going to rebuild their house. They'll stay in Coal Grove with Richie's grandma while he looks for a job. Richie's moving away."

CHAPTER 70

FOR LUCK

G us put his hand on Pete's shoulder, the way Pete had done with Richie. "Coal Grove isn't far," he said.

"Far enough. Richie's been my best friend since we were five. Now he'll go to a new school and make new friends."

Pete's words surprised Gus. Pete never lacked for friends. Gus was the shy one who'd had to wheedle his way into Pete's group. But Gus knew Richie was more than an ordinary friend.

"It won't be the same with Richie gone," Pete complained.

"I guess you're stuck with me for a best friend."

"We're not friends," Pete said. "We're brothers."

"What's wrong with being brothers *and* friends?"

"But you said we were Cain and Abel."

"That was my frustration talking," Gus tried to explain.

"Besides," Pete went on, "you'll spend all your time with Venus now that Mom and Dad are letting you." A smile began to tug at Pete's lips. "A fella can't compete with everlasting love pumping through your heart."

"That's enough of your applesauce, *Petey*."

"Go chase yourself, *Augustine*!" Pete's tone was more jest than anger. He dug something from his pocket and plunked it in Gus's hand. "If you're going to spend time with a Protestant girl, you're gonna need this more than I will." He gave Gus a wink. "For luck."

For luck? Gus looked at the old bottle cap he'd turned into a Christmas ornament many years ago. The number 7 on its face was nearly worn clean off.

"I've been carrying it around for luck," Pete said. "Sort of a nudge to God to keep you and Dad safe."

Gus remembered how he used to rub that number 7 for luck. And Pete had used it to bring Gus luck. A lump formed in Gus's throat.

They both jumped out of the way as Dad drove the Buick into the driveway and eased the car into the garage. He got out, holding a paper sack from the hardware store, and called, "The garage looks nice. You boys did a good job."

Dad paused to read their sign. "Very fitting."

"Gus wrote the poem," Pete said.

"I figured as much. You have a gift, Gus."

"It was Pete's idea," Gus said, but he savored Dad's words.

"Speaking of Pete's ideas," Dad said, "they told me at the hardware about a fella who can replace the insulation in the Kelvinator. So Pete saved us some bacon by salvaging that motor."

"Or at least a place to put the bacon," Gus joked.

Dad laughed. "Once they get the smell of the Ohio out of the refrigerator, you and I can put that motor back in, Pete."

Gus waited for the pangs of jealousy that always came from Dad and Pete doing things without him. But he didn't feel a single twinge. Working with greasy tools wasn't his idea of fun. He hated wearing filthy, sweaty clothes. He didn't want blisters and calluses when he held hands with Venus.

And he didn't need a lucky bottle cap to feel blessed. His parents loved him. They'd given their approval for him to see Venus, for crying out loud! He'd survived the Ohio River's worst flood in spite of all the strange places he'd bedded down. And meeting David had made him see the world with different eyes. Best of all, Pete still cared about him, even after Gus had ignored and antagonized him.

Dad and Pete headed inside, but Gus called Pete back and slipped the bottle cap into his hand. "I think I already have more than my share of luck," he told Pete. "You keep this. Who knows? Maybe you can use it to bring Richie's family some luck."

Pete looked ready to refuse, but grinned a *thank you* to Gus before he scrunched his eyes shut and rubbed the bottle cap vigorously.

"Maybe Richie's dad will find a new job in Ironton," Gus said. Pete flipped the bottle cap in the air, caught it, and slid it into his pocket.

AUTHOR'S NOTE

The house on Ironton's Fifth Street where my father grew up. The photo was taken during the 1937 flood by their neighbor, Paul Hill, from his porch roof across the street. He gave the photo and negative to the Cannon family in 1937.

The Brinkmeyer family is fictional, but Ironton, Ohio, is a real place—the place where my father grew up.

Floods were common in this Ohio River town, especially in Ironton's low-lying areas, where many families stayed prepared by keeping rowboats handy. Schools close to the river had trapdoors in their basements that could be opened to intentionally flood those basements and equalize pressure with floodwaters to keep foundations from collapsing.

The flood of 1937 is the worst recorded flood in the Ohio River Valley, affecting cities and towns all along the Ohio River, from Pittsburgh, Pennsylvania, to Cairo, Illinois, and on into the Mississippi River. My hometown of Cincinnati was ravaged, with the river cresting at nearly twenty-eight feet above flood stage.

In Ironton, a warmer-than-usual January quickly melted December's snow and added to snowmelt from upriver to begin the early stages of the flood. But it was the torrential rain lasting at least ten days that sealed the town's fate. The usual rainfall for the month of January was just over three inches. In 1937, it measured more than a foot.

The flood crested in Ironton at seventy feet, five inches, displaced more than 13,000 people from their homes (in a town of 16,621), and caused at least $3 million in damage (an enormous sum in 1937 dollars). Dozens of homes were washed off their foundations.

About 75 percent of Ironton was covered by water for ten days, including 3,000 dwellings, 295 stores, twelve schools, and one hospital. The water was as deep as twenty feet in the west part of town and twelve to fifteen feet in the business district. Another 15 percent of the town suffered some water damage.

The 1937 flood claimed 385 lives in thirteen states, but none in Ironton until February 2, after the floodwater had receded. A woman was crushed when a house collapsed on her. No other Ironton deaths were linked to the flood. Russell, Kentucky, a small town across the Ohio River from Ironton had eighteen thousand homeless people and was cut off from surrounding towns by the swollen river. The American Legion there dispatched boats to rescue families and offer aid. The Ironton-Russell Bridge was still above water until the height of the flood, but access to it was cut off.

My father lived in Ironton when the flood occurred, and I chose to set this story there because I grew up hearing his reminiscences of the time. His sister, Margaret Ann, recounted her memories at the age of 93, and many cousins shared the stories their parents had told. Everyone's stories matched.

My father, his parents, and siblings lived in a house on Fifth Street, where I spent a lot of time as a child and young adult. I used that house as a model for the Brinkmeyer home. It even had a sunroom with a "picnic table." That house survived the flood and still stands today.

Like Al and Ruth Brinkmeyer, my grandparents built their home on Fifth Street in 1923 to avoid flood damage

My father, Albert Cannon, evacuated his parents and siblings by rowboat from their Fifth Street home during the 1937 flood.

My grandparents, Albert and Augusta Cannon, with their children. They built their home on Ironton's Fifth Street in 1923 because they believed a flood could never reach it there.

like what had occurred in the Great Flood of 1913. Yet the 1937 flood filled their first floor with four feet, two inches of water. (Way up on Fifth Street!) They moved most of their possessions to the second floor as the river rose, but they lost a cherished player piano.

Much of what happens to the Brinkmeyers in this book is based on what actually happened to my father and his family.

Two of my aunts woke up one morning to find rowboats parked in their front yard, and Margaret Ann said the boatmen's language was "a real education."

My dad, like Gus, was reported missing, and the radio put out calls for him for two or three days. He had gone with two uncles to check on livestock at a farm owned by one of them. He returned home with a rowboat and, wearing "hip boots," rescued his family, carrying his mother and each of his siblings from their second-floor stairs to the boat.

My dad also removed the motor from their Kelvinator refrigerator and moved it upstairs to protect it from damage. When the floodwater receded, the motor was fine, but the refrigerator stunk from its insulation being saturated by filthy, muddy water. My aunt says they had it professionally cleaned and were able to continue using it.

The radio news Pete and his mother listen to, businesses closing or moving, buildings collapsing, is all true. Even the radio playing hymns so listeners could pray. Mail service was suspended for a week, and both local newspapers shut down for a week. At the height of the flood, the only working telephone in Ironton was in the courthouse, and was manned by Enoch Allen.

On January 28, Peter A. Burke and James L. Smith, using equipment in the Board of Education offices, wrote, published, and distributed what turned out to be a single edition of *The Flood Journal* to update residents on the flood's status.

The '37 flood was the impetus for flood walls in Ironton. To prevent another disaster, flood walls were constructed. The town bought six to ten feet of my grandparents' backyard, where the flood wall now passes. As a child, I played and caught lightning bugs on the grass-covered slope that was part of the flood wall.

I worked hard to get details right in this book. The movie *Klondike Annie* was playing at the Lyric Theater on Ironton's Second Street at the time of the flood. President Franklin Delano Roosevelt was inaugurated for his second term on January 20, 1937, in a "deluge." The National Guard came in to help, and food (including Wonder Bread) was donated and trucked in.

I created the character of Pete to resemble my father in many ways, though my father was actually the oldest in his family, not a younger brother. Dad was a do-it-yourself guy, but his father was not. I made up and wrote the part about Pete taking apart his grandma's cuckoo clock when he was a young boy. No one had seen that scene yet when I spoke to my aunt and asked her to tell me her memories.

By happenstance, she related a family story passed down, saying that my father took something apart (she didn't know what) at their grandma's house, and put it back together, much to everyone's amazement because he was so young. I had never heard that story before, but took it as a sign that I was telling the right story.

My dad had a widowed Aunt Mary, but I changed her last name for the book because I never met her, and most everything about the character is fiction. Dad's Aunt Mary did lose her husband to the flu epidemic of 1918–1919, and my grandpa helped her out financially. Dad's family stayed at her house when they evacuated theirs, and she housed from eighteen to twenty-two people during the flood. Margaret Ann recalls sleeping sideways, five in a bed, with her sister Rita. She and Rita were in their teens at the time, not young kids like Etta.

During the flood, Aunt Mary's visitors went to Kingsbury Elementary School to get free soup, bread, and milk, and they had to row across flooded Railroad Street to get there. They also cooked meals on an outdoor fireplace in Mary's yard. And Margaret Ann recalls they received typhoid shots, three of them.

My father's next-door neighbor, named Joe Geswein, remained in his home throughout the flood. The real-life Mr. Geswein was Dad's uncle.

My father was born into a strict Catholic family, the product of a marriage between a German Catholic and an

Irish Catholic. Their parish church, Saint Joseph, was so heavily damaged in the flood of '37 it had to be torn down. It took a dozen years to rebuild, and during that time, Sunday Mass was held in the high school gymnasium, even though there was an Irish Catholic church in town. Father Francis W. Gloekner was a real person, the pastor of Saint Joseph Church from 1915 until his death in 1939.

Dad grew up in strict adherence to his Catholic upbringing, but he married a Protestant woman. Mom converted to Catholicism when she was expecting their fourth child, and the two of them remained happily married until his death three months before their fiftieth wedding anniversary.

In 1937, the word for a child like David would have been *retarded*. Today we usually say *special needs* to cover a list of developmental problems.

Eighty years ago, children born with disabilities were put in asylums, and parents were often advised to forget the children were ever born. Like Mrs. Marlowe, many families refused to give up their children, but kept them hidden away to avoid the stigma and gossip that such a child often incurred.

Children with special needs have been a part of my life for more than fifty years. I am related to people with Down syndrome, autism, and fragile X syndrome. I have come to appreciate their uniqueness and I can't imagine a world without them.

When the flood receded and left muddy silt that needed to be cleaned away, the mud line made it obvious how high the water had reached. My Uncle Bill (my dad's younger brother) burned a mark on their garage with an electric pencil to show how high the water had risen. That mark is still there today.

My uncles, Bill and Jack Cannon, who lived in the Fifth Street house during the flood. Bill marked the garage wall to show how high the water rose.

ACKNOWLEDGMENTS

A novel is not just written. It begins as a spark of an idea, which is fanned into a story plan. That plan is researched and mapped out. Characters are created, molded, fully developed, and given voices. Scenes are drafted and built into chapters. A narrative is constructed, composed, goaded, guided, strengthened, tightened, deepened, rewritten, revised, and tweaked. I could not have done these things alone.

I owe a debt of gratitude to Kent Brown and the Highlights Foundation writers' workshops, where I learned to listen to my inner voice and hone my writing skills.

I am extremely grateful to my superb editor, Carolyn Yoder, who makes me see beyond the words to get to the heart of the story.

I thank my retreat-mates, who laugh in the right places and let me know when the story works.

I am grateful to the team at Boyds Mills Press for their support and confidence.

I have a deep appreciation for everyone who helped me plow through the flood of facts to create this work of fiction, including:

My late father, Albert Cannon, who often recounted his experiences from the '37 flood.

My aunt, Margaret Ann Henneman, who was able to recall and write pages and pages of memories, family history, and minute details of the flood of '37, despite her claims to being "not very observant" during her younger years.

Family members Sally Cannon, Tim Haney, Deb Jones, Judy Krumdieck, and KiKi Thomas-Lee, who shared photographs and passed-down memories.

The folks in the Hamner Room of Briggs Lawrence County Library in Ironton, Ohio, for sharing the flood information from their archives.

My husband, electrician Jim Wiechman, who answered my questions about all things electrical and mechanical, and who always provides a strong foundation.

I must also thank:

My first readers, Reene Clark, Nora MacFarlane, Jennifer Sommer, Rebecca Turney, and Tracy VonderBrink for their incredible feedback on a work in progress.

My critique-group members for their comments, encouragement, and unsinkable support.

PICTURE CREDITS